The Harrowed Heart

ROBERT DWIGHT BROWN

The Harrowed Heart

FULL COLOR & ILLUSTRATED - RED LETTER EDITION
With the Words our Lord and Saviour in Red
& God the Father in Purple
& the Spurious Words Attributed to Christ in Green

Anonymous Books
A Division of Chi Xi Stigma Publishing Company, LLC

Dedicated to the Remix (and Sampling) Masters
From DJ Kool Herc & Grandmaster Flash
To Jam Master Jay, Dr. Dre & Q-Tip
Through your inspiration, I create my
Literary and Biblical Remix (and Sample)

Allonymous Books

A Division of Chi Xi Stigma Publishing Company, LLC

Trade Paperback— ISBN 13: 978-1-931608-48-0

Also Available: *The First Exorcist* / *The Harrowing of the Inferno*
— ISBN 13: 978-1-931608-60-2
Also Available: *The Machination of Vipers* **— ISBN 13: 978-1-931608-71-8**

Cover image: Gerner, Peter, *Crucifixion* 1537, Walters Art Museum, Baltimore, Maryland
Paper image:: http://www.myfreetextures.com/vintage-paper-texture-with-design/

The New Testament Remixed:

The art of the remixing one artist's popular song by another artist/producer or the art of "sampling" in the hip-hop parlance of the late 1970's and 80's is lost on most people whom were not reared in the housing projects of the Bronx and other New York City boroughs. There block parties were hosted by the legendary likes of DJ Kool Herc, gave birth to an art-form predicated on the taking of the percussion "breaks" from one record and mixing it with the "breaks" of another record. This became known as sampling. As hip-hop evolved, so did the technology, allowing producers to take elements of various songs and mixing them together to make an entirely new song. This has proven to be highly controversial in the music industry (despite, or because of the profitability of the new work). The art of sampling continues to line the coffers of lawyers who argue the multitudinous lawsuits over copyright infringement. Where does one person's art (and property) end and another's art (and property) begin? That is one of the great questions raised by the rise of hip-hop.

Alan Moore's *The League of Extraordinary Gentlemen,* a series of comic-book miniseries, is a **remix (or sampling)** of literary main characters from novels *Dracula, King Solomon's Mines, 20,000 Leagues Under the Sea, The Strange Case of Dr. Jekyll and Mr. Hyde, The Invisible Man, Orlando: A Biography,* and *Carnacki the Ghost-Finder* (all fallen into the public domain, conveniently).

The Holy Bible by its very structure is a literary **remix (or sampling)**. It's sixty-six books (according to Protestant Reformers) are each the individual works of human authors (howbeit a single divine Author). Each of the books stand on their own as individual works, but only when bound together into the **remix** called the Holy Bible, do they transcend the written word to become the Word of **God**.

The Old Testament is itself a **remix** of Hebrew oral and written traditions and foreign mythologies. The Torah, once believed to be the work of a single author, namely Moses, is actually a **remix** of the independent authorships of the Jahwist, the Elohist, the Deuteronomist, and the Priestly sources. The other authors of the Old Testament took entire stories, prayers, and covenants from other older Hebrew scripture and freely inserted them into their own books, sometimes with nary a change to be found. Was this outright theft? Or was it a divine remix?

The New Testament is also an abuser of this type of divine literary remix. The Gospels of Matthew and Luke have been rightly accused by the most esteemed Biblical scholars over the centuries to have plagiarized wantonly the Gospel of Mark and the mysterious Q-"Gospel", creating three "synoptic" Gospels out of an original two (one having been forever lost to history). Only John's Gospel escapes this abuse of remix by writing an inherently original and at times throughout history, questioned Gospel. So much for originality.

Doubt me?

Choose any Study Bible worth its salt and you will discover a column of scriptural references for practically every verse in the entirety of the Old and New Testaments. While some of these references are merely thematic in nature, many are paraphrased and often direct quotations of other, older scripture. This is the nature of The Holy Bible: the Divine Remix.

Need I continue?

If Jesus, as many Atheists assert, was the fictional creation of his "followers", then the authors of the New Testament made the Gospel of "Jesus of Nazareth" a remix of the Messianic prophecies of their Hebrew scripture. If Jesus was either a historical person or the divine, then His ministry is a remix of Old Testament and wholly (Holy) original belief systems.

Could I take the texts of the Gospels of Matthew, Mark, Luke, and John and by cutting and pasting scriptures wantonly here and there, compose a truly original work? A horror novel?

Hell, yeah!

Danse Macabre: To the modern reader, horror fiction began with Edgar Allen Poe continued to the weird supernatural fiction of H.P. Lovecraft and the horror of Richard Mattheson, Shirley Jackson, and Ray Bradbury, and concludes in the modern era with Stephen King. But *Danse Macabre* ("the Dance of Death") dates the horror genre to, at least, the Late Middle Ages through art, allegory, and music. But being scared by stories, no doubt, dates back to the primordial past with Cro-Magnon man sitting around the fire retelling the harrowing hunting of mammoths.

But *Why* focus a retelling and re-imagining of the Gospel narrative as a horror novel? Shouldn't the Gospel narrative uplift, inspire, and demand devotion?

Is this why most of the masters of horror, have shied away from the Gospel narrative, or Christianity as a source of their horror? H.P. Lovecraft devoted himself to creating his own weird Cthulhu Mythos, most horror novels (and movies) are surprisingly agnostic. Sure, William Peter Blatty shocked readers and Hollywood audience members with *The Exorcist*, a novel (and subsequent movie) that brought an obscure Catholic rite into the mainstream light. I'm sure Protestants and non-religious alike are scared by the movie (and novel), but this a work designed to truly scare, terrify, and horrify Catholics.

The French film *Martyrs,* begins as a classic (if not horrifying) revenge movie, before morphing into testicle-clinching torture-porn. Yet, in the literal final moments of the motion picture, *Martyrs* reveals itself to be a truly transcendent religious experience. How could a movie of such shocking and revolting violence be transcendent? I love *Martyrs* as one of my all-time favorite films and I cannot answer this question, nor can I watch it *ever* again. It is that disturbing.

And speaking of disturbing torture-porn: Mel Gibson's shocking and shockingly successful *The Passion of the Christ* took a passionate and myopic view of the suffering of Jesus Christ through His arrest, scourging, and crucifixion. As I sat in the theater awaiting the movie to begin, there were several groups of Christians each with their own minister preparing their congregations for the message of the movie: (which apparently is) that Jesus suffered and died for their sins. When the credits rolled and as the congregations of Christians wept for His suffering, I sat stunned by my enjoyment of such an exquisite horror movie. This is not a film in the tradition of Cecil B. DeMille, but Eli Roth. *The Passion* is classic 21st Century torture-porn.

When I decided that I wanted to finally write a horror novel in the vein of Stephen King, Clive Barker, or William Peter Blatty, what subject would I focus on? Slashers, demons, vampires, werewolves, ghosts, zombies? There are so many wonderful sub-genres to horror fiction, the possibilities seemed endless.

As I began preparing my mind for the grueling undertaking of writing a truly terrifying horror novel, I knew a few things. I wanted it to be based on a religious experience (not unlike *The Exorcist*), but one that hadn't been done to death (like *The Exorcist*). Then a disturbing thought occurred to me. One of the most horrifying scriptures I ever read as a young Catholic, one that haunted my dreams and caused many nights of nightmares was: *when Jesus asked a man with an unclean spirit, "What is thy name?" And he answered, saying, "My name is Legion: for we are many."* (Mk. 5:9). I knew because of this scripture and a certain other scripture (Mt. 27:52-53) that *The Harrowed Heart* and *The First Exorcist* (ISBN 13: 978-1-931608-60-2) would include two of the great tropes of horror fiction: exorcisms and zombies!

"Wait! What? There may be exorcisms in the Gospel narrative", you say, **"but there certainly aren't mother-f***ing zombies!"**

Of course there are!

Then *the graves were opened; and many bodies of the saints which slept arose, and after Jesus' resurrection, when they had come out of the tombs, they entered the holy city and appeared to many people* (Mt. 27:52-53)!

I had my answer! I could focus the Gospel narrative, and ratchet up the suspense, mystery, terror, shock, and gore but include exorcisms and mother-fucking zombies, amongst many other classic horror tropes, including a descent into Hell itself!

Why would you ever doubt me?

Author's Note:
False Writings & False Witnesses:

To the early Christian church, eyewitness testimony to the life and ministry of Jesus the Christ were of utmost importance when selecting their sacred texts. *Forasmuch as many have taken in hand to set forth in order a declaration of those things which are most surely believed among us, Even as they delivered them unto us, which from the beginning were eyewitnesses, and ministers of the word; It seemed good to me also, having had perfect understanding of all things from the very first, to write unto thee in order, most excellent Theophilus, That thou mightest know the certainty of those things, wherein thou hast been instructed* (Lk. 1:1-4).

Many Biblical scholars and laypersons, including Dan Brown, author of *The DaVinci Code*, hypothesize that The Holy Bible wasn't set in stone until the First Council of Nicea in A.D. 325, but this is a falsehood and creative rewriting of early church history. Modern writers and some scholars delight in the early Church waging a war to the very death over canonical and non-canonical scripture, popular and unpopular Jesus narratives, and sacred and spurious gospels. But the early Church Fathers had already established a canon of authentic sacred scripture early in the second century, mere decades after the Gospels of Mark, Matthew, Luke, and John were written between A.D. 50 and 90. This was a era in human history where oral tradition was the main source of passing down history and sacred knowledge. Oral tradition is surprisingly accurate and often without error, but the permanent recording of the Gospels in the new technology of the codex (in Greek no less) was quick and remarkably forward thinking of the Evangelists.

Still in the second century, Marcion of Sinope, who believed himself to be an Early Church Father, sought to supplant the established canon with his own, that included many other "Gnostic gospels" and dismissed the entirety of the Old Testament. With the discovery of the Nag Hammadi library of codices, modern Christians and septics for the first time in centuries have access to this Gnostic knowledge. But the writings are spurious and late additions that championed a Christian philosophy that could not survive the centuries, and certainly not Constantine's conversion to Christianity.

Over the course of the centuries many other gospels were written: Jewish-Christian gospels, Infancy gospels, "lost" gospels, and medieval gospels. In the last two centuries there has been an explosion of spurious "modern" gospels: *The Aquarian Gospel of Jesus Christ*, *The Book of Mormon*, *The Fifth Gospel*, *The Gospel of Satan*, and *The Urantia Book*. These books are certainly far too late to be the party to be considered canonical, historically accurate, or even respectable books. Even *my own*, damn near two-thousand years too late, **The Holy Bible Trilogy: The Old, New & Next Testaments** (ISBN 13: 978-1-931608-49-7) purports to be an authentic, "God-breathed", canonical sequel to the Old and New Testaments (which it *is*).

So where does *The Harrowed Heart* sit in comparison to the four Canonical Gospels? My book certainly does nothing of the sort. My so-called **"New Testament Remixed"** is more akin to the Hollywood Biblical Epics that took cinematic narratives and set them in the time and place of Jesus of Nazareth of Galilee. While set 1,300 years before Christ, Cecil B. Demille brought *The Ten Commandments* to the cinemas twice, once in the silent era and the other in the Technicolor one staring Charlton Heston. *Ben-Hur* directed by William Wyler and staring, again, Charlton Heston, tells a story that runs parallel with the Gospel Narrative until the two eventually intersect. The Richard Burton starring-vehicle *The Robe* tells a post-Gospel Narrative about the Roman centurion who gambled for and won Jesus' robe and eventually coverts to this new sect.

Call *The Harrowed Heart* a **"novelization"** of the Gospels and I'll accept it. Call *The Harrowed Heart* a **"cutting-and-pasting"** of The Holy Bible and I'll begrudgingly acquiesce. But I'll defend my **"New Testament Remixed"** as a work of (perhaps) great import: **the Good News for the 21st Century** & **a Biblical Epic that will scare the Hell out of you scare Heaven into you.**

Chapter 1
"In The Garden"

HE HAD FALLEN WITH HIS FACE upon the ground, clutching at the soft, moist dirt of the Garden known as Gethsemane. A skin-crawling insect with a hundred-most-unnatural-legs, who hath made its home in the soft, moist, and welcoming soil, wiggled out of the knot of dirt in His fist. And yet He suffered nary any fright as the dozens of *Sicarii*-legs of the repugnant insect prickling and tickling the skin of His hand as it sought its own escape from death. The prickling sent the lightest flashes of lightning up His spine, causing His shoulders to shudder and His face to wince, but His distress distracted Him. He released the clumps to rain down upon the earth. Lo! The pest scurried away disappearing into the fallen leaves of under-brush. He seized then another fistful of earth, the veins bulging and throbbing on the backs of His hands and His blood seeped

1

out from underneath **His** nails.

　　He knew the words of John, son of Elizabeth, whom was the cousin of **His** Mother Mary, when he saith, "Behold the **Lamb of God**, which taketh away the sin of the world. This is **He** of whom I said, 'After me cometh a **Man** which is preferred before me: for **He** was before me.' And I knew **Him** not: but that **He** should be made manifest to Israel, therefore am I come baptizing with water."

　　He knew **He** manifested to take away our sins; and in **Him** is no sin. Whosoever abideth in **Him** sinneth not: whosoever sinneth hath not seen **Him**, neither known **Him**. Little children, shalt let no man deceive them: he that doeth righteousness is righteous, even as **He** is righteous. He that committeth sin is of the devil; for the devil sinneth from the beginning. For this purpose the **Son of God** manifested, that **He** might destroy the works of the devil.

　　"O! My Father, if it be possible, let this cup pass from Me: nevertheless not as I will, but as thou wilt." Thus He fulfilled the prophesy, the **Lord GOD** hath opened **His** ear, and **He** was not rebellious, neither turned away back. For who in the days of **His** flesh, when **He** had offered up prayers and supplications with strong crying and tears unto **Him** that was able to save **Him** from death, and was heard in that **He** feared; though **He** were a **Son**, yet learned **He** obedience by the things which **He** suffered; and being made perfect, **He** became the author of eternal salvation unto all them that obey **Him**; called of **God** an high priest after the order of Melchisedec.

　　Howbeit, **His** heart harrowed knowing **The End** neared and upon **Him** was a journey to the cross and the unimaginable suffering of the servant. **He** hath come unto Jerusalem, and now must suffer many things and be rejected of the elders and chief priests and scribes, and be nailed to the cross after being scourged of His flesh, His flesh striped and shredded into strips of flesh by the whips of knots and bone. To die upon the cross, to be displayed like meat in a bazaar for the onlookers and gawkers, left to hang for days until the overwhelming exhaustion causes His lungs to lengthen and His legs to weaken so He can no longer draw any measure of breath, His heart to strain in the pain, and to finally die. But! after three days He shall rise again, howbeit, calm the war-beat of the drum of His harrowed heart the Holy Ghost could not.

He buried His face in the damp earth, the grass and moss tickling His beard, as He breathed in dank earthy fragrances, His Divine tears irrigated the soil with a holy water the roots were most unaccustomed to. What kind of blessing would such tears of sorrow bring the tenderest of shoots? Lo! He wept with woe, His breath shuddering, His chest heaving, His stomach quivering. He wailed like a infant-child into the cool bosom of the earth with prayers to the very heights of heaven. In His anguish, He sang a Psalm of David:

"My God, My God, why hast Thou forsaken Me? Why art Thou so far from helping Me, and from the words of My roaring? O! My God, I cry in the day time, but Thou hearest not; and in the night season, and am not silent.

"But thou art holy, O! Thou that inhabitest the praises of Israel. Our fathers trusted in Thee: they trusted, and Thou didst deliver them. They cried unto Thee, and were delivered: they trusted in Thee, and were not confounded.

"But I am a worm, and no man; a reproach of men, and despised of the people. All they that see Me laugh

Me to scorn: they shoot out the lip, they shake the head, saying, 'He trusted on the Lord that He would deliver Him: let him deliver Him, seeing he delighted in Him.'

"But Thou art He that took Me out of the womb: thou didst make Me hope when I was upon My mother's breasts. I was cast upon Thee from the womb: Thou art My God from My mother's belly. Be not far from Me; for trouble is near; for there is none to help.

"Many bulls have compassed Me: strong bulls of Bashan have beset Me round. They gaped upon Me with their mouths, as a ravening and a roaring lion.

"I am poured out like water, and all My bones are out of joint: My heart is like wax; it is melted in the midst of My bowels. My strength is dried up like a potsherd; and My tongue cleaveth to My jaws; and thou hast brought Me into the dust of death.

"For dogs have compassed Me: the assembly of the wicked have inclosed Me: they pierced My hands and My feet. I may tell all My bones: they look and stare upon Me. They part My garments among them, and cast lots upon My vesture.

"But be not Thou far from Me, O! Lord: O! My strength, haste Thee to help Me."

He knew, most certainly He did, what was going to come to pass in the next sprinkling of hours and on the morrow and the day after to-morrow. His Father had written, breathing in breathes of the long dead Prophets, the very Prophecies that were to be fulfilled, not in some unknowable and incalculable future, but in a few, very short hours. His fellow Israelites had been awaiting the fulfilment of the Prophecies concerning the coming of the Messiah for precisely twenty-four score-and-six and yet, this generation would not pass away until all had been fulfilled.

His hour is come, finally come, that the Son of man should be glorified. Verily, verily, He hath said these very words unto His Disciples, "Except a corn of wheat fall into the ground and die, it abideth alone: but if it die, it bringeth forth much fruit. He that loveth his life shall lose it; and he that hateth his life in this world shall keep it unto life eternal. If any man serve Me, let him follow Me; and where I am, there shall also My servant be: if any man serve Me, him will My Father honour.

"Now is My soul troubled; and what shall I say? Father, save Me from this hour: but for this cause came I unto this hour. Father, glorify Thy name.

"Then came there a voice from heaven, saying, 'I have both glorified it, and will glorify it again.' "

The people therefore, that hath once stood by, and heard it, said that it thundered: others said, "An angel spake to Him."

He hath answered and said, "This voice came not because of Me, but for your sakes. Now is the judgment of this world: now shall the prince of this world be cast out. And I, if I be lifted up from the earth, will draw all men unto Me." This He said, signifying what death He should die.

The people hath answered Him, "We have heard out of the law that Christ abideth for ever: and how sayest Thou, the Son of man must be lifted up? Who is this Son of man?"

Then He said unto them, "Yet a little while is the light with you. Walk while ye have the light, lest darkness come upon you: for he that walketh in darkness knoweth not whither he goeth. While ye have light, believe in the light, that ye may be the children of light." These things spake **He**, and departed, and did hide himself from them.

Daniel the Prophet, in court of Nebuchadnezzar of Babylon, hath once prophesied, "Seventy weeks are determined upon thy people and upon thy holy city, to finish the transgression, and to make an end of sins, and to make reconciliation for iniquity, and to bring in everlasting righteousness, and to seal up the vision and prophecy, and to anoint the most **Holy**. Know therefore and understand, that from the going forth of the commandment to restore and to build Jerusalem unto the **Messiah the Prince** shall be seven weeks, and threescore and two weeks: the street shall be built again, and the wall, even in troublous times. And after threescore and two weeks shall **Messiah** be cut off, but not for **Himself**: and the people of the prince that shall come shall destroy the city and the sanctuary; and the end thereof shall be with a flood, and unto the end of the war desolations are determined. And He shall confirm the covenant with many for one week: and in the midst of the week **He** shall cause the sacrifice and the oblation to cease, and for the overspreading of abominations **He** shall make it desolate, even until the consummation, and that determined shall be poured upon the desolate."

If instead of weeks of days, they were days of years, indeed then **He** knew and the scribes of the Temple knew, that Daniel's prophecy should fulfil itself this very year. Not only did **He** await this very week of days to fulfil the prophecy, as did the elders and the chief priests and the scribes, whom feared their hold over the grip on Israel no longer was on the wax, but on the wane. But little did the Sanhedrin comprehend their seeking how they might kill **Him** (for they feared the people and for they feared **Him**, because they had made the calculations and knoweth the Messiah lived and walked amongst them), aligned with His own devices for He must also suffer for sins, the just for the unjust, that He might bring us to God, being put to death in the flesh, but quickened by the Spirit.

He had once taught His disciples, "But of that day and hour knoweth no man, no, not the angels of heaven, but My Father" So, assuredly, He knew that day and hour for He had set the events into motion not unlike a Commander of a Roman Legion sets his plans of battle to siege a walled-city. Had He not found in the temple those that sold oxen and sheep and doves, and the changers of money sitting: in the shadow of the Holiest of Holies, the very seat of His Father on the Earth? Had He not made a scourge of small cords? Had He not driven them all out of the temple, and the sheep, and the oxen; and poured out the changers' money, and overthrew the tables? Had He not said unto them that sold doves, "Take these things hence; make not My Father's house an house of merchandise!"?

Woe! back in the moment in the garden, a smile curled through the anguish that distorted the features of His face. He had found the courage to scourge the Sanhedrin, to lay a challenge their authority over the people of Judaea and the Galilee, but the murder of crows had proven to be a crowd of cowards, not wishing to affront Rome's authority by having arrested this mad messiah, who was known to wander with a smattering of disciples from the city of Jerusalem and the wilderness in the surrounding Judaea and in the most distant rural villages of the Galilee. With the reports from their network of spies and informants, a meagre cabal of the Sanhedrin believed this was not a Messiah whom assembled an army to overthrow the yoke of Rome. This rural Rabbi was nothing but a Messiah who warned, through parables and platitudes, of the coming of the kingdom of God. His disciples were fishermen and prostitutes preaching peace and prosperity to the poorest of the poor. Bah! It was a humbug! I humbug I tell you! This Man, the meagre cabal argued, was no great and mean threat to Rome and therefore was no great and mean threat to the Sanhedrin's authority over the multitudes. But what if He could be proven to be a threat? This Saul of Tarsus wouldst argue before Caiaphas, the High-Priest, and the assembly of Pharisees and Sadducees. Lo! Then this knowledge would require a different tact, much more bloody tact than a blind dismissal.

But He knew the heart of His treasurer, Judas Iscariot; He knew Judas desired not to be a disciple of the Suffering Servant, but a Militaristic Messiah that would overthrow the rule of Rome with an army of disciples, turning the waters of the river Jordan red with blood, not with the rod of Aaron, howbeit with the sword. Judas went his way, and communed with the chief priests and captains, how he might betray Him unto them. And they were glad, and covenanted to give him money. And he promised, and sought opportunity to betray Him unto them in the absence of the multitude. The Sanhedrin would be rid of yet another false messiah who tempted the foolish poor into dismissing their own teachings and authority into believing myths of the coming of a Kingdom of God. To the elders and the chief priests and the scribes, Jesus of Nazareth of the Galilee was nothing but bothersome gnat that buzzed in their faces, but did them no real harm. However to Nicodemus, He was the Son of God.

The Sanhedrin knew the true reality of God. Certainly they did. They were His authorized agents, priests of politics. God was, of course, nothing more a fictional phantasm that gave them wealth and authority in eyes of the people and kept the people plying their trades and paying their tithes. The Holy of Holies contained nothing. Their scriptures were nothing but folk stories, but as the Word of God, they were a collar and chain that burdened the people into servitude. What was thirty pieces of silver compared to the spectacle of the crucifixion of a **false messiah** who dared challenge their authority and their coin-purse by that theatre in the Temple?

He knew the heart of Judas that His treasurer desired not a mere thirty pieces of silver, but to provoke this Messiah into sedition and messiahship. To call upon the Jerusalemites that had welcomed Him to the celebration of the Feast of Passover in Jerusalem, the City of David, by spreading their garments in the way; others cutting down branches from the trees, and strawing them in the way. And the multitudes that went before, and that followed, cried, saying, "Hosanna to the son of David: Blessed is He that cometh in the name of the LORD; Hosanna in the highest."

And when He was come into Jerusalem, all the city was moved, saying, "Who is this?" And the multitude said, "This is Jesus the prophet of Nazareth of Galilee."

In Judas' hopes and dreams, these great multitudes, all of the city, whom welcomed Him into Jerusalem as the Messiah, would rise up when Jesus, from Nazareth of Galilee, would be found illegally arrested during the Feast of Passover and together all of the city would overthrow Pontius Pilate, the governor of Roman province of Judaea and a Procurator of Rome. Only when the narrow streets of Jerusalem were then cleansed of the pagan urine and faeces of the Caesar with the blood of the Roman Legions. This faith warmed the heart of Judas Iscariot and was the reason why he betrayed Him.

He comforted **Himself** in this knowledge that Judas betrayed **Him** at this very moment to the Sanhedrin for thirty pieces of silver, at **His** request. During the last supper **He** would share with **His** Apostles, **He** troubled in spirit, and testified, **"Verily I say unto you, that one of you shall betray Me."**

Then the disciples looked one on another, doubting of whom **He** spake. Now there leaning on **His** bosom one of **His** disciples, whom **He** loved. Simon Peter therefore beckoned to **Him**, that he should ask who it should be of whom **He** spake. The beloved disciple then lying on **His** breast saith unto **Him**, **"Lord**, who is it?"

And **He** answered and said, **"He that dippeth his hand with Me in the dish, the same shall betray Me. The Son of man goeth as it is written of Him: but woe unto that man by whom the Son of man is betrayed! It had been good for that man if he had not been born."**

Then Judas, which betrayed **Him**, answered and said, "Master, is it I?"

Then said **He** unto him, **"That thou doest, do quickly."**

Now no man at the table knew for what intent **He** spake this unto him. For some of them thought, because Judas had the bag, that **He** had said unto him, "Buy those things that we have need of against the feast; or, that he should give something to the poor." **He** then having received the sop went immediately out: and it was night.

But now, **He** could feel the anger of the Sanhedrin rolling down the streets of Jerusalem like an ominous fog. **He** knew the loyal guards of the Sanhedrin would be coming armed with swords and clubs. No one else in the city

---

*The disciples sleep while **He** is in agony in the garden, whilst **He** begs, **"Let this cup pass from me: nevertheless not as I will, but as thou wilt"**!*

knew they were not staying at an inn in the city or up in the countryside, but had made their camp in the Garden of Gethsemane. His disciples believed they were safe there, but He knew differently. He knew a spy in their midst had betrayed their camp to the authorities whom were now on the move.

Back in the moment of serene safety of the garden, He pulled himself to His feet, brushed the moist dirt from His face and beard. Wiping His tears from His cheeks, He stumbled, intoxicated on anguish, back to where the disciples had staid to watch with Him. His muscles were weak and His heart and lungs exhausted from His weeping and His agony. He came to the camp of His disciples, and found them sleeping, and He cried to Peter, the Rock on which He would build His Church, "What, could ye not watch with Me one hour? Watch and pray, that ye enter not into temptation: the spirit indeed is willing, but the flesh is weak.

"Heed ye not My teaching of prophecy and foreboding? When I saith, 'Behold, we go up to Jerusalem; and the Son of man shall be betrayed unto the chief priests and unto the scribes, and they shall condemn Him to death, and shall deliver Him to the Gentiles to mock, and to scourge, and to crucify Him: and the third day He shall rise again?' "

And in his sleep, Peter rebuked Him, murmuring, "Be it far from Thee, Lord: this shall not be unto Thee."

"Get thee behind Me, Satan: thou art an offence unto Me: for thou savourest not the things that be of God, but those that be of men."

Then He said unto His still slumbering disciples His grief growing, "If any man will come after Me, let him deny himself, and take up his cross, and follow Me.

For whosoever will save his life shall lose it: and whosoever will lose his life for My sake shall find it. For what is a man profited, if he shall gain the whole world, and lose his own soul? or what shall a man give in exchange for his soul? For the Son of man shall come in the glory of His Father with his angels; and then He shall reward every man according to his works. Verily I say unto you, 'There be some standing here, which shall not taste of death, till they see the Son of man coming in His kingdom.' "

Again, a second time as He went away, and several score of serpents slithered from the brush, all cursed by God like that old serpent, called the Devil and their sire, Satan, who art cursed above all cattle, and above every beast of the field; upon their belly shalt they go, and dust shalt they eat all the days of their life: And the LORD hath put enmity between them and the woman, and between their seed and her seed; He shall bruise their head, and they shalt bruise His heel. And the score of serpents then slunk away from Him disappearing into the underbrush.

And then He fell upon a large stone, cold and comforting, and safe and secure. He clutched the stone as if it were the hull of a capsized boat in the Sea of Galilee. He was unable to quiet the great tempest in the sea that arose on the sea of His sorrow, as He had once done when rebuked the winds and the sea, and there was a great calm. But the men marvelled, saying, "What manner of Man is this, that even the winds and the sea obey Him!" But this great storm He could not weather. The pouring rains were His tears and the howling winds were His wailing breath, and His sorrow were the waves thrashing the boat upon the rocks. The wailing waves swept over the boat and He drowned in sorrow.

He clasped His hands together in both supplication

and submission, with such a carpenter's strength that the bones of His hands screamed that they were afraid of breaking, the veins throbbed with the thunderous pulse of His harrowed heart, **"O! My Father, if it be possible, let this cup pass from Me: nevertheless not as I will, but as Thou wilt."**

He knew the punishment for claiming to be a Messiah was death. He knew there was also a false messiah called Simon of Peraea, who had been a slave of king Herod, but in other respects a comely person, of a tall and robust body; he was one that was much superior to others of his order, and had had great things committed to his care. This man was elevated at the disorderly state of things, and was so bold as to put a diadem on his head, while a certain number of the people stood by him, and by them he was declared to be a king, and he thought himself more worthy of that dignity than any one else.

Simon of Peraea burnt down the royal palace at Jericho, and plundered what was left in it. He also set fire to many other of the king's houses in several places of the country, utterly destroyed them, and permitted those that were with him to take what was left in them for a prey. He would have done greater things, but care was taken to repress him immediately. The commander of Herod's infantry, Gratus joined himself to some Roman soldiers, took the forces he had with him, and met Simon. And after a great and a long fight, no small part of those that had come from Peraea (a disordered body of men, fighting rather in a bold than in a skilful manner) were destroyed. Although Simon had saved himself by flying away through a certain valley, Gratus overtook him, and cut off his head.[1]

All knoweth the punishment for sedition was cruci-

---

1 Flavius Josephus, *Jewish War* 2.57-59 and *Jewish Antiquities* 17.273-277

fixion. He had seen with His eyes crucifixions. All of Judaea and Galilee, from men to their women and their babes, had come upon criminals crucified like an orchard on their journeys along the roads and upon the hills surrounding the city of David. Even the babes dreamth nightmares in the small hours. This was how blessedly commonplace the crucifixion of criminals was. The bodies of the dead, left upon the tree after their bodies had shuddered their last breath, to be torn apart by wild dogs. The dying also left upon the crosses, their cries, their pain, their suffering, a warning from Rome to the Israelites to pay their taxes, to obey Roman law, and certainly, most assuredly never contemplate sedition. The fowls cared not if the criminal still breathed in laboured breaths to feast upon their eyes and on the more tender and personal bits, for the Roman Centurions also cared not for the modesty of the condemned nor that the LORD hath commanded: His body shall not remain all night upon the tree, but thou shalt in any wise bury Him that day; (for he that is hanged is accursed of God;) that thy land be not defiled, which the LORD thy God giveth thee for an inheritance.

He knew He could have helped the crucified. It was within His power and His authority from His Father to have ordered the condemned off the cross and the criminal would have obeyed, despite and in spite of the iron nails and the stout wood, much to the awe and wonderment (and punishment) of the Centurions guarding the damned. The wounds of their scourging and the damage from the iron nails pierced and pounded into their wrists and their ankles could be healed if He spat on the ground and made a clay with His spittle. But He knew that a single life saved from crucifixion was incomparable to His own Atonement on the cross. He Who His own self bare our sins in His own body on the tree, that we, being dead to sins, should live unto righteousness: by whose stripes ye were healed.

Continued reciting His Psalm of David did He, "But be not Thou far from Me, O! Lord: O! My strength, haste Thee to help Me. Deliver My soul from the sword; My darling from the power of the dog. Save Me from the lion's mouth: for Thou hast heard Me from the horns of the unicorns.

"You have answered Me.

"I will declare Thy name unto My brethren: in the midst of the congregation will I praise thee. Ye that fear the Lord, praise Him; all ye the seed of Jacob, glorify Him; and fear Him, all ye the seed of Israel. For He hath not despised nor abhorred the affliction of the afflicted; neither hath He hid his face from Him; but when He cried unto Him, He heard."

He came again and found them sleeping, for their eyes were heavy. "So, could you not keep watch with Me one hour? Watch and pray that you enter not into temptation. The spirit indeed is willing, but the flesh is weak. For the hour is come, that the Son of man should be glorified. Verily, verily, I say unto you, 'Except a corn of wheat fall into the ground and die, it abideth alone: but if it die, it bringeth forth much fruit.' " He left them again, and went away wary and weeping, and prayed a third time, saying the same words, "O! My Father, if it be possible, let this cup pass from Me: nevertheless not as I will, but as Thou wilt."

His tears overflowed His eyes, flooding down the lines in His face like the river Nile when Moses lifted up the rod, and smote the waters that were in the river, in the sight of Pharaoh, and in the sight of his servants; and all the waters that were in the river were turned to blood. Such was His agony, **His** anguish, that **He** no longer shed tears, **He** bled tears.

And concluded the sings of the Psalm of David did **He**, **"My praise shall be of Thee in the great congregation: I will pay My vows before them that fear Him. The meek shall eat and be satisfied: they shall praise the Lord that seek Him: your heart shall live for ever.**

"All the ends of the world shall remember and turn unto the Lord: and all the kindreds of the nations shall worship before Thee. For the kingdom is the Lord's: and he is the governor among the nations.

"All they that be fat upon earth shall eat and worship: all they that go down to the dust shall bow before Him: and none can keep alive his own soul. A seed shall serve Him; it shall be accounted to the Lord for a generation.

"They shall come, and shall declare His righteousness unto a people that shall be born, that He hath done this."

He raised **His** head from supplication and submission, and there beaded on **His** forehead were drops of blood. **He** wiped **His** forehead with the sleeve of **His** robe, a fine robe, the finest of white robes without seam, woven from the top throughout. The sleeve of **His** robe now stained with the sweat of **His** blood.

Then cometh **He** to **His** disciples, and saith unto them, **"Sleep on now, and take your rest: behold, the hour is at hand, and the Son of man is betrayed into the hands of sinners. Rise, let us be going: behold, he is at hand that doth betray Me."**

And Judas also, which betrayed **Him**, knew the place: for **He** ofttimes resorted thither with **His** disciples. Judas then, having received a band of men and officers from the elders and chief priests and scribes, cometh into the darkness of the garden armed with lanterns and torches and weapons.

And immediately, while **He** yet spake, cometh Judas, one of the twelve, and with him a great multitude with swords and staves, assigned and consigned in their duties. And he that betrayed **Him** had given them a token, saying, "Whomsoever I shall kiss, that same is **He**; take **Him**, and lead **Him** away safely."

He therefore, knowing all things that should come upon him, went forth, and said unto them, **"Whom seek ye?"**

The soldiers of the Sanhedrin answered **Him**, **"Jesus of Nazareth of the Galilee."** **He** saith unto them, **"I AM He"**. And Judas also, which betrayed **Him**, stood with them. As soon then as **He** had said unto them, **"I AM He"**, they went backward, and fell to the ground.

Then asked **He** them again, **"Whom seek ye?"** And they said, **"Jesus of Nazareth."** **He** answered, **"I have told you that I AM he: if therefore ye seek Me, let these go their way"**: That the saying might be fulfilled, which **God** spake, **"Of them which Thou gavest Me have I lost none."**

And as soon as Judas was come, he goeth straightway to **Him**, and saith, **"Hail, master"**; and kissed **Him**. Lo! Faithful are the wounds of a friend; but the kisses of an enemy are deceitful. Woe! **He** said unto him, **"Friend, wherefore art thou come?"** Then came the soliders, and laid hands on **Him** and took **Him** so that it may be fulfilled of the Prophets: **"Yea! Mine own familiar friend, in whom**

Judas betrays **Him** *with a kiss!*

I trusted, which did eat of My bread, hath lifted up his heel against Me."

And, behold, then Simon Peter having a sword hung at his waiste, drew it, and smote the high priest's servant, and smote off his right ear. The servant's name was Malchus. The flesh of his hearing fell upon the dirt of the earth and blood poured down his cheek upon his neck and upon his breast. He dropped to his knees, not in supplication to **Him**, but unto shock and fear. He put his hand upon the wound and looked into **His** eyes as if to say, "Ye, O! **Jesus of Nazareth of the Galilee**, I hath heard reports of **Thy** fulfilleth the Prophecy of Isaiah, whom saith, 'Then the eyes of the blind shall be opened, and the ears of the deaf shall be unstopped. Then shall the lame man leap as an hart, and the tongue of the dumb sing: for in the wilderness shall waters break out, and streams in the desert."

Then said **He** unto Simon Peter, **"Put up again thy sword into his place: the cup which My Father hath given Me, shall I not drink it? Woe! unto thee, Simon, he that leadeth into captivity shall go into captivity: he that killeth with the sword must be killed with the sword. Here is the patience and the faith of the saints. Woe! to thee that spoilest, and thou wast not spoiled; and dealest treacherously, and they dealt not treacherously with thee! when thou shalt cease to spoil, thou shalt be spoiled; and when thou shalt make an end to deal treacherously, they shall deal treacherously with thee. Thinkest thou that I cannot now pray to My Father, and He shall presently give Me more than twelve legions of angels? But how then shall the scriptures that I prayeth this night be fulfilled, that thus it must be?"**

And **He** spat on the flesh of Malchus' hearing which layeth on the ground, and made clay of the spittle, and **He** anointed the smotten ear and restored it unto Malchus.

In that same hour He said to the multitudes, "Are ye come out as against a thief with swords and staves for to take Me? I sat daily with you teaching in the temple, and ye laid no hold on Me. But all this was done, that the scriptures of the prophets might be fulfilled."

And despite, Nay! in spite of, the miracle they all witnessed, the a band of men and officers from the chief priests and scribes, cometh thither pummelling Him and smote Him blackening His eyes, and loosening His teeth. The thunder of their blows echoed through the serene and eerily quite of the garden of Gethsemene frightening the birds into flight and the dogs into their howling. They lashed Him with chains of unearthly weight, that strained and tore the muscles in His shoulders, shoulders which they beat with their bludgeons. They mauled Him! They manhandled Him! They sought to hand Him over to their earthly lords, the elders and the chief priests and the scribes of the Sanhedrin.

He spat His blood, the blood of a New Covenant, upon the moist soil of the ground, which maketh not peace, for it is not yet the blood the cross. He wept, not in pain, but knowing that soon, justified by His blood, we shall be saved from wrath through Him. He wept in fear that He mayeth die in the garden and not upon the cross: if not through His own blood which a death here granteth not eternal redemption, whom God hath set forth to be a propitiation through faith in His blood, to declare His righteousness for the remission of sins that are past, through the forbearance of God. Still! oh! Father, LORD God of Israel! Shall it be still only by the blood the blood of bulls and of goats, and

the ashes of an heifer sprinkling the unclean, sanctifieth to the purifying of the flesh? O! Woe! how much
more shall **His** Blood, who through the eternal **Spirit**
offered himself without spot to **God**, purge your conscience from dead works to serve the living **God**? And for
this cause **He** must be the mediator of the new testament,
that by means of death, for the redemption of the transgressions that were under the first testament, they which
are called might receive the promise of eternal inheritance.

Then all **His** disciples forsook **Him** and their nets as
fishers of men; knowing the fate of messiahs is crucifixion
and the fate of the disciples of the crucified messiahs is surely a similar death. So in their fear, which quickened their
breath and thundered their hearts, they fled into the shadows cast by Satan himself. ✝

Chapter 2
"The Forbidden Trial"
Part the First

HE **CONSPIRACY AGAINST JE-sus of Nazareth of the Galilee** reached its penultimate the night before suffering **His** agony in the Garden of Gethsemane, when the Pharisees and Sadducees argued in a secret and nocturnal and forbidden trial before Caiaphas and the Sanhedrin.

The chief priests and the scribes the same hour sought to lay hands on **Him**; and they feared the people: for they perceived that **He** had spoken this parable against them: "**A certain man planted a vineyard, and let it forth to husbandmen, and went into a far country for a long time. And at the season he sent a servant to the husbandmen, that they should give him of the fruit of the vineyard: but the husbandmen beat him, and sent him away empty. And again he sent another servant: and they beat him also, and entreated him shamefully, and sent him away**

empty. And again he sent a third: and they wounded him also, and cast him out. Then said the lord of the vineyard, 'What shall I do? I will send My beloved son: it may be they will reverence him when they see him.'

"But when the husbandmen saw him, they reasoned among themselves, saying, this is the heir: come, let us kill him, that the inheritance may be ours. So they cast him out of the vineyard, and killed him. What therefore shall the lord of the vineyard do unto them? He shall come and destroy these husbandmen, and shall give the vineyard to others."

So the Sanhedrin watched Him, and sent forth spies, which should feign themselves just men, that they might take hold of His words, that so they might deliver Him unto the power and authority of the governor: Pontius Pilate. Wide was the knowledge of vindictiveness and furious temper of the governor, who is naturally inflexible, a blend of self-will and relentlessness and his corruption, and his acts of insolence, and his rapine, and his habit of insulting people, and his cruelty, and his continual murders of people untried and uncondemned, and his never ending, and gratuitous, and most grievous inhumanity[1]

The first of the many spies, a witness to His control of nature, testified, "And the apostles, when they were returned, told Him all that they had done. And He took them, and went aside privately into a desert place belonging to the city called Bethsaida. And the people, when they knew it, followed Him: and He received them, and spake unto them of the kingdom of God, and healed them that had need of healing. And when the day began to wear away, then came the twelve, and said unto Him, 'Send the multitude away,

---

1 Philo, *On The Embassy of Gauis* Book XXXVIII

that they may go into the towns and country round about, and lodge, and get victuals: for we are here in a desert place.'

"But **He** said unto them, **'Give ye them to eat.'** And they said, 'We have no more but five loaves and two fishes; except we should go and buy meat for all this people.' For they were about five thousand men.

"And **He** said to **His** disciples, **'Make them sit down by fifties in a company.'** And they did so, and made them all sit down. Then **He** took the five loaves and the two fishes, and looking up to heaven, **He** blessed them, and brake, and gave to the disciples to set before the multitude. And they did eat, and were all filled: and there was taken up of fragments that remained to them twelve baskets."

Another of their multitude of spies, a witness to **His** healing of the leper, declared, "And there came a leper to **Him**, beseeching **Him**, and kneeling down to **Him**, and saying unto **Him**, 'If thou wilt, thou canst make me clean.'

"And **He**, moved with compassion, put forth **His** hand, and touched him, and saith unto him, **'I will; be thou clean.'** And as soon as **He** had spoken, immediately the leprosy departed from **Him**, and **He** cleansed him. And **He** straitly charged him, and forthwith sent him away; and saith unto him, **'See thou say nothing to any man: but go thy way, shew thyself to the priest, and offer for thy cleansing those things which Moses commanded, for a testimony unto them.'** "

But the third spy, a witness to **His** healing of the blind, swore, "And they came to Jericho: and as **He** went out of Jericho with **His** disciples and a great number of people, blind Bartimaeus, the son of Timaeus, sat by the highway side begging. And when he heard that it was **Jesus of Nazareth of the Galilee**, he began to cry out, and say, **'Jesus,**

Thou son of David, have mercy on me.' And many charged him that he should hold his peace: but he cried the more a great deal, 'Thou son of David, have mercy on me.'

"And He stood still, and commanded him to be called. And they called the blind man, saying unto him, 'Be of good comfort, rise; He calleth thee.'

"And he, casting away his garment, rose, and came to Him. And He answered and said unto him, 'What wilt thou that I should do unto thee?' The blind man said unto him, 'Lord, that I might receive my sight.'

"And He said unto him, 'Go thy way; thy faith hath made thee whole.' And immediately he received his sight, and followed Him in the way."

Howbeit another spy, a witness to His casting out of demons, affirmed, "And they came over unto the other side of the sea, into the country of the Gadarenes. And when He was come out of the ship, immediately there met Him out of the tombs a man with an unclean spirit, who had his dwelling among the tombs; and no man could bind him, no, not with chains: because that he had been often bound with fetters and chains, and the chains had been plucked asunder by him, and the fetters broken in pieces: neither could any man tame him. And always, night and day, he was in the mountains, and in the tombs, crying, and cutting himself with stones.

"But when he saw Him afar off, he ran and worshipped him, and cried with a loud voice, and said, "What have I to do with thee, Jesus, thou Son of the most high God? I adjure thee by God, that Thou torment me not." For He said unto him, 'Come out of the man, thou unclean spirit.'

"And He asked him, "What is thy name?" And he answered, saying, 'My name is Legion: for we are many.'

And he besought **Him** much that he would not send them away out of the country. Now there was there nigh unto the mountains a great herd of swine feeding. And all the devils besought him, saying, 'Send us into the swine, that we may enter into them.' And forthwith **He** gave them leave. And the unclean spirits went out, and entered into the swine: and the herd ran violently down a steep place into the sea, (they were about two thousand;) and were choked in the sea.

"And they that fed the swine fled, and told it in the city, and in the country. And they went out to see what it was that was done. And they come to **Him** and see him that was possessed with the devil, and had the legion, sitting, and clothed, and in his right mind: and they were afraid. And they that saw it told them how it befell to him that was possessed with the devil, and also concerning the swine. And they began to pray him to depart out of their coasts."

And cometh forward a final spy, a witness to the resurrection of the dead, who corroborated, "Behold, there came a man named Jairus, and he was a ruler of the synagogue: and he fell down at **His** feet, and besought **Him** that he would come into his house: for he had one only daughter, about twelve years of age, and she lay a dying. While he yet spake, there cometh one from the ruler of the synagogue's house, saying to him, 'Thy daughter is dead; trouble not the **Master**.'

"But when **He** heard it, **He** answered him, saying, **'Fear not: believe only, and she shall be made whole.'** And when **He** came into the house, **He** suffered no man to go in, save Peter, and James, and John, and the father and the mother of the maiden. And all wept, and bewailed her: but he said, **'Weep not; she is not dead, but sleepeth.'**

"And they laughed **Him** to scorn, knowing that she was

dead. And **He** put them all out, and took her by the hand, and called, saying, *'Talitha cumi'*, which is interpreted as 'Maid, arise!' And her spirit came again, and she arose straightway: and **He** commanded to give her meat. And her parents were astonished: but **He** charged them that they should tell no man what was done."

Then gathered the chief priests and the Pharisees a council, and saith, "What do we? For this **Man** doeth many miracles. If we let **Him** thus alone, all men will believe on **Him**: and the Romans shall come and take away both our place and nation."

And one of them, named Caiaphas, being the high priest that same year, said unto them, "Ye know nothing at all, nor consider that it is expedient for us, that one **Man** should die for the people, and that the whole nation perish not."

A Pharisee stepped forward to defend **Him**, for he was a secret disciple to **Jesus of Nazareth of the Galilee**. The Sanhedrin knew not this truth, but Nicodemus sought to defend his **Rabbi**, his **Messiah**, "Now I am a man of the Pharisees named Nicodemus, a ruler of the Jews. I came to **Him** by night, and said unto **Him**, '**Rabbi**, we know that **Thou** art a teacher come from **God**: for no man can do these miracles that **Thou** doest, except **God** be with **Him**.'

"**He** answered and said unto me, '**Verily, verily, I say unto thee, except a man be born again, he cannot see the kingdom of God.**'

"And I saith unto **Him**, 'How can a man be born when he is old? Can he enter the second time into his mother's womb, and be born?'

He answered, '**Verily, verily, I say unto thee, except a man be born of water and of the Spirit, he cannot enter**

Nicodemus the Pharisee becomes Born Again and a secret disciple of **His**!

into the kingdom of God. That which is born of the flesh is flesh; and that which is born of the Spirit is spirit. Marvel not that I said unto thee, ye must be born again. The wind bloweth where it listeth, and thou hearest the sound thereof, but canst not tell whence it cometh, and whither it goeth: so is every one that is born of the Spirit.'

"And I answered and said unto **Him**, 'How can these things be?' **He** answered and said unto me, '**Art thou a master of Israel, and knowest not these things?** Verily, verily, I say unto thee, we speak that we do know, and testify that we have seen; and ye receive not our witness. If I have told you earthly things, and ye believe not, how shall ye believe, if I tell you of heavenly things? And no man hath ascended up to heaven, but He that came down from heaven, even the Son of man which is in heaven. And as Moses lifted up the serpent in the wilderness, even so must the Son of man be lifted up: that whosoever believeth in Him should not perish, but have eternal life. For God so loved the world, that He gave His only begotten Son, that whosoever believeth in Him should not perish, but have everlasting life. For God sent not His Son into the world to condemn the world; but that the world through Him might be saved.

" 'He that believeth on Him is not condemned: but he that believeth not is condemned already, because he hath not believed in the name of the only begotten Son of God. And this is the condemnation, that light is come into the world, and men loved darkness rather than light, because their deeds were evil. For every one that doeth evil hateth the light, neither cometh to the light, lest his deeds should be reproved. But he that doeth truth

Saul brings false witnesses before Caiaphas in his house!

cometh to the light, that his deeds may be made
manifest, that they are wrought in God.' "

Saul of Tarsus, circumcised the eighth day, of the
stock of Israel, of the tribe of Benjamin, an Hebrew of
the Hebrews; as touching the law, a Pharisee; concerning
zeal, persecuting the ministry; touching the righteousness
which is in the law, blameless, then argued, "Answereth
me! How can **God the Father** be the **Son** and the **Spirit**? I
tell you, **God** is One! For **God** spake, **'I AM the Lord, and
there is none else, there is no God beside Me: I girded
thee, though thou hast not known Me: That they may
know from the rising of the sun, and from the west, that
there is none beside me. I AM the Lord, and there is none
else.'**

"**God** is the **LORD** and there is no other. **Jesus**, the
false prophet, but is Satan's brother. There can never be a
Holy Trinity! **Jesus**! The **Son of God**, is but insanity."

Nicodemus presented a prophecy, "Daniel the Dreamer, saith once, 'Seventy weeks are determined upon thy people and upon thy holy city, to finish the transgression, and
to make an end of sins, and to make reconciliation for iniquity, and to bring in everlasting righteousness, and to seal
up the vision and prophecy, and to anoint the most **Holy**.
Know therefore and understand, that from the going forth
of the commandment to restore and to build Jerusalem unto
the **Messiah** the **Prince** shall be seven weeks, and threescore
and two weeks: the street shall be built again, and the wall,
even in troublous times. And after threescore and two weeks
shall **Messiah** be cut off, but not for **Himself**: and the people of the **Prince** that shall come shall destroy the city and
the sanctuary; and the end thereof shall be with a flood, and
unto the end of the war desolations are determined. And
He shall confirm the covenant with many for one week: and

in the midst of the week **He** shall cause the sacrifice and the oblation to cease, and for the overspreading of abominations **He** shall make it desolate, even until the consummation, and that determined shall be poured upon the desolate.' Blind folly-fallen Pharisees," Nicodemus pleadeth, "We art days of seven from whence the **LORD** our **God** shalt restore Heaven!"

"Pharisees, have thee of thy faith rescued!" Saul exclaimed, "Our fair Nicodemus hath told untruths; thy faith our brother askews. The Prophets hath foretold the **Messiah**! The **Nazarene** is not whom is expected by us!

" 'And **He** shall set up an ensign for the nations,' saith Isaiah, 'and shall assemble the outcasts of Israel, and gather together the dispersed of Judah from the four corners of the earth.'

"And likewise saith Isaiah, 'And it shall come to pass in that day, that the **LORD** shall beat off from the channel of the river unto the stream of Egypt, and ye shall be gathered one by one, O! ye children of Israel. And it shall come to pass in that day, that the great trumpet shall be blown, and they shall come which were ready to perish in the land of Assyria, and the outcasts in the land of Egypt, and shall worship the **LORD** in the holy mount at Jerusalem.'

"**He** is not the Messiah, whom the Prophets hath foretold. We a scattered people are. **His** lies are quite bold!"

Counter Nicodemus did, "Did the **Rabbi** not say, **'Think not that I am come to destroy the law, or the prophets: I am not come to destroy, but to fulfil.'**

"These are the Messiah's accomplishments: Micah spake, 'Bethlehem Ephratah, though thou be little among the thousands of Judah, yet out of thee shall **He** come forth unto **Me** that is to be ruler in Israel; whose goings forth have been from of old, from everlasting. For the son dishonoureth the father, the daughter riseth up against her mother, the daughter in law against her mother in law; a man's enemies are the men of his own house.' "

"Bah!" Saul cursed, "When didst Jesus of Nazareth of the Galilee fulfil the prophecy of Michah?"

And Nicodemus answereth, "Now when Jesus was born in Bethlehem of Judaea in the days of Herod the king, behold, there came wise men from the east to Jerusalem. And they said unto him, 'In Bethlehem of Judaea: for thus it is written by the prophet, and thou Bethlehem, in the land of Juda, art not the least among the princes of Juda: for out of thee shall come a Governor, that shall rule my people Israel.' And for Jesus saith, 'Think not that I am come to send peace on earth: I came not to send peace, but a sword. For I am come to set a man at variance against his father, and the daughter against her mother, and the daughter in law against her mother in law.'

"And then Malachi spake, 'Behold, I will send you Elijah the prophet before the coming of the great and dreadful day of the Lord: Behold, I will send my messenger, and he shall prepare the way before Me: and the Lord, whom ye seek, shall suddenly come to His temple, even the messenger of the covenant, whom ye delight in.' "

"Fie!" cursed did Saul, "When didst Jesus of Nazareth of the Galilee fulfil the prophecy of Malachi?"

And Nicodemus answereth, "In the beginning was the Word, and the Word was with God, and the Word was God. And the Word was made flesh, and dwelt among us, (and we beheld His glory, the glory as of the only begotten of the Father,) full of grace and truth.

"And! As they departed, He began to say unto the multitudes concerning John, 'What went ye out into the wilderness to see? A reed shaken with the wind? But what went ye out for to see? A man clothed in soft raiment? Behold, they that wear soft clothing are in kings' houses. But what went ye out for to see? A prophet? Yea, I say unto you, and more than a prophet. For this is he, of whom it is written, "Behold, I send My messenger before thy face, which shall prepare thy way before thee. Verily I say unto you." Among them that are born of women there hath not risen a greater than John the Baptist: notwithstanding he that is least in the kingdom of heaven is greater than he.'

"And Isaiah then spake, 'For unto us a child is born, unto us a son is given: and the government shall be upon His shoulder: and His name shall be called Wonderful, Counsellor, The Mighty God, The Everlasting Father, The Prince of Peace. Of the increase of His government and peace there shall be no end, upon the throne of David, and upon His kingdom, to order it, and to establish it with judgment and with justice from henceforth even for ever. The zeal of the LORD of hosts will perform this.' "

"How, how," Saul cursed, "When didst Jesus of Nazareth of the Galilee fulfil the prophecy of Isaiah?"

And Nicodemus answereth again, "The book of the generation of Jesus Christ, the son of David, the son of Abraham. Abraham begat Isaac; and Isaac begat Jacob; and Jacob begat Judas and his brethren; and Judas begat Phares and Zara of Thamar; and Phares begat Esrom; and Esrom begat Aram; and Aram begat Aminadab; and Aminadab begat Naasson; and Naasson begat Salmon; and Salmon begat Booz of Rachab; and Booz begat Obed of Ruth; and Obed begat Jesse; and Jesse begat David the king; and David the king begat Solomon of her that had been the wife of Urias; and Solomon begat Roboam; and Roboam begat Abia; and Abia begat Asa; and Asa begat Josaphat; and

Josaphat begat Joram; and Joram begat Ozias; and Ozias begat Joatham; and Joatham begat Achaz; and Achaz begat Ezekias; and Ezekias begat Manasses; and Manasses begat Amon; and Amon begat Josias; and Josias begat Jechonias and his brethren, about the time they were carried away to Babylon: and after they were brought to Babylon, Jechonias begat Salathiel; and Salathiel begat Zorobabel; and Zorobabel begat Abiud; and Abiud begat Eliakim; and Eliakim begat Azor; and Azor begat Sadoc; and Sadoc begat Achim; and Achim begat Eliud; and Eliud begat Eleazar; and Eleazar begat Matthan; and Matthan begat Jacob; and Jacob begat Joseph the husband of Mary, of whom was born Jesus, who is called Christ. So all the generations from Abraham to David are fourteen generations; and from David until the carrying away into Babylon are fourteen generations; and from the carrying away into Babylon unto Christ are fourteen generations.

"And Isaiah continueth the Prophecy, 'Therefore the LORD himself shall give you a sign; behold, a virgin shall conceive, and bear a Son, and shall call His name Immanuel.' "

"Bah! It is a Humbug!" Saul cursed, "When didst Jesus of Nazareth of the Galilee fulfil this second prophecy of Isaiah?"

And Nicodemus obliged, "Now the birth of Jesus Christ was on this wise: when as His mother Mary was espoused to Joseph, before they came together, he found her with Child of the Holy Ghost. Behold, a virgin shall be with child, and shall bring forth a son, and they shall call His name Emmanuel, which being interpreted is, God with us."

"Howbeit," Saul protested, "First, the prophet Isaiah, seven centuries from this prophecy and thirty years hence,

Joseph, Mary's husband, being a just man, and not willing to make her a public example, minded to put her away privily. But while he thought on these things, behold, the angel of the **LORD**, according to the gossiping of hens, appeared unto him in a dream, saying, 'Joseph, thou son of David, fear not to take unto thee Mary thy wife: for that which is conceived in her is of the Holy Ghost.' And she shall bring forth a son, and thou shalt call **His** name **JESUS**: for **He** shall save **His** people from their sins. **His** name is **JESUS** not IMMANUEL! Should not this counterfeit 'angel of the **LORD**' have instructed Joseph, the carpenter of Nazareth of the Galilee, to name his son 'Immanuel'? Why do these hens gossip under the guise of prophecies? How in the name of the **Blessed** is this prophecy fulfilled by **Jesus of Nazareth of the Galilee**? It is not! It can not be!"

" 'Behold,' " Nicodemus continued neglecting the argument of Saul, "Isaiah prophecied, 'I lay in Zion for a foundation a stone, a tried stone, a precious corner stone, a sure foundation: he that believeth shall not make haste. And he shall be for a sanctuary; but for a stone of stumbling and for a rock of offence to both the houses of Israel, for a gin and for a snare to the inhabitants of Jerusalem. And many among them shall stumble, and fall, and be broken, and be snared, and be taken.'"

"Bah! It is a Humbug!" Saul cursed, "When didst **Jesus of Nazareth of the Galilee** fulfil this third prophecy of Isaiah?"

And Nicodemus saith the words of **Jesus** saith unto **His** disciples, **"Did ye never read in the scriptures, 'The stone which the builders rejected, the same is become the head of the corner: this is the Lord's doing, and it is marvellous in our eyes?'**

"And Isaiah likewise saith, 'Nevertheless the dimness shall not be such as was in her vexation, when at the first **He** lightly afflicted the land of Zebulun and the land of Naphtali, and afterward did more grievously afflict her by the way of the sea, beyond Jordan, in Galilee of the nations. **He** is despised and rejected of men; a man of sorrows, and acquainted with grief: and we hid as it were our faces from **Him**; **He** was despised, and we esteemed **Him** not.

"When!" Saul cursed yet again, ""Didst **Jesus of Nazareth of the Galilee** fulfil this fourth prophecy of Isaiah?"

And Nicodemus saith the words of **Jesus** whom saith unto **His** disciples, " '**The Son of man must suffer many things, and be rejected of the elders and chief priests and scribes, and be slain, and be raised the third day.**' But first must **He** suffer many things, and be rejected of this generation.

"And Isaiah continueth his Prophecies," continueth Nicodemus, " 'The **Spirit** of the **LORD God** is upon me; because the **LORD** hath anointed me to preach good tidings unto the meek; **He** hath sent me to bind up the brokenhearted, to proclaim liberty to the captives, and the opening of the prison to them that are bound. To appoint unto them that mourn in Zion, to give unto them beauty for ashes, the oil of joy for mourning, the garment of praise for the spirit of heaviness; that they might be called trees of righteousness, the planting of the **LORD**, that **He** might be glorified.'

"Fie!" cursed did Saul, "Oh merciful **LORD**, when didst **Jesus of Nazareth of the Galilee** fulfil the fifth prophecy of Isaiah?"

And Nicodemus again saith, "The blind receive their sight, and the lame walk, the lepers are cleansed, and the deaf hear, the dead are raised up, and the poor have the gospel preached to them. And Jeremiah spake, 'Thus saith the LORD, "A voice was heard in Ramah, lamentation, and bitter weeping; Rahel weeping for her children refused to be comforted for her children, because they were not." ' "

Weary, Saul cried, full of frustration, "When didst Jesus of Nazareth of the Galilee fulfil this prophecy of Jeremiah?"

And Nicodemus recalled the whispers of the past, "Then Herod, when he saw that he was mocked of the wise men, was exceeding wroth, and sent forth, and slew all the children that were in Bethlehem, and in all the coasts thereof, from two years old and under, according to the time which he had diligently inquired of the wise men.

"And Zechariah spake, 'Rejoice greatly, O! daughter of Zion shout: O! daughter of Jerusalem: Behold, thy King cometh unto thee: He is just, and having salvation; lowly, and riding upon an ass, and upon a colt the foal of an ass. If ye think good, give me my price; and if not, forbear. So they weighed for my price thirty pieces of silver.' "

And Saul sighed with great lamentations exhausted from the counsel of Nicodemus. He dropped upon his knees and wept with vexing and clawed upon the tiled stones of the palace of Caiaphas like unto a mongrel dog. How could every Prophecy foretelling the Messiah be fulfilled in this Jesus of Nazareth of the Galilee? The LORD God created no numbers high enough to figure the odds that He alone fulfilled all of the Prophecies concerning the Coming of the Messiah. Bah! It was a humbug! This Jesus of Nazareth of the Galilee was no— could be no— Messiah!

And Nicodemus answereth the silent, exasperated challenge from Saul, "This fulfilled when the disciples of Jesus of Nazareth of the Galilee** went, and did as **Jesus** commanded them, and brought the ass, and the colt, and put on them their clothes, and they set **Him** thereon. And a very great multitude spread their garments in the way; others cut down branches from the trees, and strawed them in the way. And the multitudes that went before, and that followed, cried, saying, 'Hosanna to the son of David: Blessed is **He** that cometh in the name of the **LORD**; Hosanna in the highest.' "

A fire kindled in the clouded heart of Saul upon hearing the supposed fulfilment of Zechairah's Prophecy, "Howbeit canst a Prophecy be counted as fulfilled when **He** commanded the fulfilment of said Prophecy? **He** is a learned Rabbi. Knoweth the scriptures well does **He**! Orchestrated the fulfilment of the Prophecies of the Prophets! Micah is offended! Malachi is outraged! Isaiah and Zechariah art insulted and defamed! This **Jesus of Nazareth of the Galilee** is a charlatan and a liar both!"

Nicodemus opened his mouth to speak, to answer, to defend his **Rabbi**, but Saul of Tarsus continueth with great mockery, "Hath **He** risen against Rome, overthrown the eagle? Should not this professed **Messiah** judge among the nations, and rebuke many people: and we shall beat our swords into plowshares, and our spears into pruninghooks: nation shall not lift up sword against nation, neither shall they learn war any more. Hath Rome's oppression for peace, we mistook? The **Messiah** shalt the Word of **God** spread. The YHWH shalt be king of all creation! And the gods of foreign lands to the dead. One day shalt be one **LORD** and **His** name one!"

"Howbeit," Nicodemus declared, "The Nazarene these prophecies, hath **He** not fulfilled. **He** be youthful. Fulfill these might **He** still. Is **He** not a prophet of the **LORD** like

Elias."

Saul in his raging saith, "Prophecy can exist, only riseth, when our land hath contained all the world's Jewry; the death of Malachi ended the age of prophecy: Ezekial saith, 'My tabernacle also shall be with them: yea, I will be their God, and they shall be my people. And the heathen shall know that I the LORD do sanctify Israel, when my sanctuary shall be in the midst of them for ever-more.'

"Didst Herod not restore upon the land the place of Solomon," continueth Saul, "Is Herod the Messiah we fawn on? Nay! Faith! Howbeit, Herod maketh peace with our enemies and returneth Jewry to our sanctuary. He was not and is not our Messiah! Though God liveth in the Holy of Holies, this prophecy is but Herod's solely. Is not Herod, by decree of the Roman Mongrels, the 'King of the Jews'. Why art thou not agog! Worship thee not the massacrer of innocents?' "

"Fie!" Nicodemus cried, "O! Scribe, ye twist the LORD's word. Fulfillment, He is, of the Holy Word of God!"

"Bah!" Saul revolted, "Forewarned art we that there arise among us a prophet, or a dreamer of dreams, and giveth thee a sign or a wonder, and the sign or the wonder come to pass, whereof He spake unto thee, saying, 'Let us go after other gods, which thou hast not known, and let us serve them'; thou shalt not hearken unto the words of that prophet, or that dreamer of dreams: for the LORD your God proveth you, to know whether ye love the LORD your God with all your heart and with all your soul. Ye shall walk after the LORD your God, and fear Him, and keep His commandments, and obey His voice, and ye shall serve him, and cleave unto Him. And that prophet, or that dreamer

of dreams, shall be put to death; because **He** hath spoken to turn you away from the **LORD** your **God**, which brought you out of the land of Egypt, and redeemed you out of the house of bondage, to thrust thee out of the way which the **LORD** thy **God** commanded thee to walk in. So shalt thou put the evil away from the midst of thee.

"If thy brother, the son of thy mother, or thy son, or thy daughter, or the wife of thy bosom, or thy friend, which is as thine own soul, entice thee secretly, saying, 'Let us go and serve other gods', which thou hast not known, thou, nor thy fathers; namely, of the gods of the people which are round about you, nigh unto thee, or far off from thee, from the one end of the earth even unto the other end of the earth; thou shalt not consent unto **Him**, nor hearken unto **Him**; neither shall thine eye pity **Him**, neither shalt thou spare, neither shalt thou conceal **Him**: but thou shalt surely kill **Him**; thine hand shall be first upon **Him** to put **Him** to death, and afterwards the hand of all the people.

"And thou shalt stone **Him** with stones shalt he die! The **LORD** thy **God** brought thee from Egypt land; to the Romans must he be crucified!"

Heretofore after the trial had finished, Saul of Tarsus returneth to his inn where he stayeth whilst in celebration of the season of Passover and met in the darkest of corners in conspiracy of Judas Iscariot. In a neighbouring doorway, a prostitute committeth immoralities with her mouth and drinketh the salacious sinful seed of Moloch. And in the distant darkness, a pick-thief murdered most malevolently a merchant returning to his home and his family for the Feast. *Drachma*, bearing the image and superscription of Caesar, scattered on the stones like rats fleeing the light of a torch from his fallen purse.

Judas, the disciple to **Jesus of Nazareth of the Galilee**, proffered a justification of his betraying his Rabbi and Master, "From the shadows, thy debate I hath heard. Yesternight whilst the disciples slumbered, **He** took me aside and saith, 'Come, Secrets may I teach ye no man knoweth or hath e'er seen. Exists there a great, boundless Realm, no generation of angels knoweth or hath seen, wherefrom cometh a great and Invisible Spirit no thought of heart hath ever comprehended and hath by Name never called. There materialized a cloud of great light that saith, "Let an Angel cometh into being as My Houseman." The Houseman, Self-Begotten Enlightened-divine, issued from the cloud a' four angels sprang from some other cloud And they grew into housemen. The Houseman saith, "Letteth angels come into Being to serveth Him, and myriads Of no known number came into being." He saith, "An aeon enlightened shalt come into being and he cameth into Being." A second luminary reigned over him, with myriads of angels without known number. Adamas is the Name of the first luminous cloud ere no Angel amongst them calleth God who maketh seventy-two luminaries of the incorruptible generation, wherefore each hath three hundred sixty luminaires appeareth unto the same generation, in accordance with the will of the Spirit. The twelve aeons of twelve luminaries constitute their father of six heavens for each aeon. Seventy-two heavens. Seventy-two luminaries. For each of them five firmaments totaling three hundred sixty firmaments. Given Authority over a great host of Angels with nary a known number for glory and adoration of virgin Spirits for glory and adoration of all the aeons and the heavens and their firmaments. This great multitude of those immortals calleth the cosmos or perdition by O! The great Father, the luminaries and the aeaons. In Him appeareth the first man and the Angel called El saith, "Let twelve angels cometh into being to rule over chaos. From the cloud cameth an angel flashed with fire and defiled with blood named Nebro which the others calleth him Yaldabaoth. Another, Saklas, cometh forth from the cloud. Nebro called Saklas to be His houseman And twelve angels claimed their twelve hides of land of heaven. Twelve kings spake with twelve angels, the first is Seth, who shalt be called the Christ. The second is Harmathoth, the third Galila, The fourth Yobel, the fifth Adonaios. Art these five rule over Hades and the First of all over chaos. Then Saklas saith to his angels, "Letteth us in the Likeness and image create us humans." Adam was fashioned as was his wife Eve, Calleth in the cloud, Zoe.'"

"I asketh Jesus, 'Doth the human spirit die?"

"To which Jesus saith, 'Why this is God ordered Michael to giveth the spirits of man as usury, so they shouldst offer service, however The Great One commandeth Gabriel to bequeath spirits to the great generation with nary a ruler to rule o'er it – That is the spirit and the soul. But God affected knowledge of Good and Evil to be bequeathed to Adam and the men with him, so the kings of chaos and Hades shalt not lord o'er them'

"I queried Him, 'So what will those these generations do?' Verily, He chortled at me. 'Master,' I saith, 'why art Thou chortling me.'

" 'Verily,' He saith, 'I chortle not at ye but at the

Judas agrees to betray Him for thirty pieces of silver, the potter's price!

err of the many stars. Verily these six stars wander about with five enemies and they all shalt be ruined along with their creatures. Verily, I say to you, "Judas, you will exceed all of them. For you will sacrifice the Man that bare Me. Since he will be destroyed. The image of the great generation of Adam shalt be exalted, for prior to heaven, earth, and the angels of that Generation which is from the eternal Realms, exists." Look, you hath been told e'erything. Lift thy eyes and looketh at the cloud and the light held within and the surrounding Stars. The star that leadeth thy way is your star. Ye shalt becometh the thirteenth a' ye shalt Be cursed by the other generations – And ye shalt cometh to rule o'er them all.' "[2]

Saul resteth a comforting hand upon the weary and wary shoulders of the Betrayer, and saith, "Judas! Friend! Let us conspire to retire a' retire to conspire."

And thus was fulfilled the Prophecy of the Shepherd of Zechariah: thus saith the LORD my God; "Feed the flock of the slaughter; whose possessors slay them, and hold themselves not guilty: and they that sell them say, 'Blessed be the LORD; for I am rich': and their own shepherds pity them not. For I will no more pity the inhabitants of the land, saith the LORD: but, lo, I will deliver the men every one into his neighbour's hand, and into the hand of his king: and they shall smite the land, and out of their hand I will not deliver them.'

---

2   The Gospel of Judas, a Gnostic gospel, late 2nd century

"And I will feed the flock of slaughter, even you, O! poor of the flock. And I took unto me two staves; the one I called Beauty, and the other I called Bands; and I fed the flock. Three shepherds also I cut off in one month; and My soul lothed them, and their soul also abhorred me. Then said I, I will not feed you: that that dieth, let it die; and that that is to be cut off, let it be cut off; and let the rest eat every one the flesh of another. And I took My staff, even Beauty, and cut it asunder, that I might break My covenant which I had made with all the people. And it was broken in that day: and so the poor of the flock that waited upon Me knew that it was the word of the LORD. And I said unto them, "If ye think good, give me my price; and if not, forbear." So they weighed for my price thirty pieces of silver.' "Cast it unto the potter: a goodly price that I was prised at of them."

And Zechariah took the thirty pieces of silver, and cast them to the potter in the house of the LORD. Then Zechariah cut asunder his other staff, even Bands, that I might break the brotherhood between Judah and Israel.

And the LORD said unto Zechariah, "Take unto thee yet the instruments of a foolish shepherd. For, lo, I will raise up a shepherd in the land, which shall not visit those that be cut off, neither shall seek the young one, nor heal that that is broken, nor feed that that standeth still: but he shall eat the flesh of the fat, and tear their claws in pieces. Woe to the idol shepherd that leaveth the flock! the sword shall be upon his arm, and upon his right eye: his arm shall be clean dried up, and his right eye shall be utterly darkened."

Chapter 3
"The Forbidden Trial"
Part the Second

AND THE SOLDIERS LED HIM away from the garden at Gethsemane to the high priest: and with him were assembled all the chief priests and the elders and the scribes. And Peter followed **Him** afar off, even into the palace of the high priest: and he sat with the servants, and warmed himself at the fire. Peter prayed in silence that **He** would heed **His** own words, when **He** hath saith on the mount, **"Agree with thine adversary quickly, whiles thou art in the way with him; lest at any time the adversary deliver thee to the judge, and the judge deliver thee to the officer, and thou be cast into prison."**

And the chief priests and all the council sought for witness against **Him** to put **Him** to death! And found none amongst the multitudes whom counted as **His** disciples or a very great multitude, whom are counted amongst the wheat

48

and not the chaff. For the wheat spread their garments in the way; others cut down branches from the trees, and strawed them in the way, saying, "Hosanna to the son of David: Blessed is He that cometh in the name of the LORD; Hosanna in the highest."

The Pharisees and Sadducees rememberth not the warnings of John the Baptizer, "O! generation of vipers, who hath warned you to flee from the wrath to come? Bring forth therefore fruits meet for repentance: And think not to say within yourselves, 'We have Abraham to our father': for I say unto you, that God is able of these stones to raise up children unto Abraham. And now also the axe is laid unto the root of the trees: therefore every tree which bringeth not forth good fruit is hewn down, and cast into the fire. I indeed baptize you with water unto repentance. But He that cometh after me is mightier than I, whose shoes I am not worthy to bear: He shall baptize you with the Holy Ghost, and with fire: whose fan is in His hand, and He will throughly purge His floor, and gather His wheat into the garner; but He will burn up the chaff with unquenchable fire."

For the LORD thy God knoweth the people of the land of Judaea and the Galilee, whom walked with Him, ate His fish and bread, listened to His Gospel and His parables are the wheat that will feed the starving and shall be sown in good ground and shall bring forth fruit, some an hundredfold, some sixtyfold, some thirtyfold. The chief priests and the elders and the scribes who now hold a council against Him, how they might destroy Him, are the chaff that they shall not be planted; yea, they shall not be sown: yea, their stock shall not take root in the earth: and He shall also blow upon them, and they shall wither, and the whirlwind shall

The gleeful husbandmen slay the servants and son of the vineyard!

take them away as stubble.

Then a venerable scribe stood and giveth his testimony before Caiaphas against Him saying, "Then began Jesus of Nazareth of the Galilee to speak to the people this parable, 'A certain man planted a vineyard, and let it forth to husbandmen, and went into a far country for a long time. And at the season he sent a servant to the husbandmen, that they should give him of the fruit of the vineyard: but the husbandmen beat him, and sent him away empty. And again he sent another servant: and they beat him also, and entreated him shamefully, and sent him away empty. And again he sent a third: and they wounded him also, and cast him out.

" 'Then said the lord of the vineyard, 'What shall I do? I will send My beloved son: it may be they will reverence him when they see him.' But when the husbandmen saw him, they reasoned among themselves, saying, 'This is the heir: come, let us kill him, that the inheritance may be ours.' So they cast him out of the vineyard, and killed him. What therefore shall the lord of the vineyard do unto them? He shall come and destroy these husbandmen, and shall give the vineyard to others. And when they heard it, they said, 'God forbid.' And he beheld them, and said, 'What is this then that is written, The stone which the builders rejected, the same is become the head of the corner'? Whosoever shall fall upon that stone shall be broken; but on whomsoever it shall fall, it will grind him to powder.' "

For Caiaphas hath known that very same hour the elders, chief priests, and scribes sought to lay hands on Him; and they feared the multitude, because they took Him for a prophet and the multitude perceived that He had spoken this parable against the Pharisees and Sanhedrin. And now it had come to pass.

And yet another esteemed scribe giveth his testimony before Caiaphas against **Him** saying, "When **Jesus of Nazareth of the Galilee** came unto the multitude, and to **His** disciples, saying '**The scribes and the Pharisees sit in Moses' seat: all therefore whatsoever they bid you observe, that observe and do; but do not ye after their works: for they say, and do not. For they bind heavy burdens and grievous to be borne, and lay them on men's shoulders; but they themselves will not move them with one of their fingers. But all their works they do for to be seen of men: they make broad their phylacteries, and enlarge the borders of their garments, and love the uppermost rooms at feasts, and the chief seats in the synagogues, and greetings in the markets, and to be called of men, 'Rabbi, Rabbi.' But be not ye called Rabbi: for one is your Master, even Christ; and all ye are brethren. And call no man your father upon the earth: for one is your Father, which is in heaven. Neither be ye called masters: for one is your Master, even Christ. But he that is greatest among you shall be your servant. And whosoever shall exalt himself shall be abased; and he that shall humble himself shall be exalted.**

" '**But woe unto you, scribes and Pharisees, hypocrites! For ye shut up the kingdom of heaven against men: for ye neither go in yourselves, neither suffer ye them that are entering to go in. Woe unto you, scribes and Pharisees, hypocrites! For ye devour widows' houses, and for a pretence make long prayer: therefore ye shall receive the greater damnation.**

" '**Woe unto you, scribes and Pharisees, hypocrites! For ye compass sea and land to make one proselyte, and**

Woe unto the elders and the chief priests and the scribes, otherwise a brood of vipers!

when he is made, ye make him twofold more the child of hell than yourselves.

" 'Woe unto you, ye blind guides, which say, "Whosoever shall swear by the temple, it is nothing; but whosoever shall swear by the gold of the temple, he is a debtor!" Ye fools and blind: for whether is greater, the gold, or the temple that sanctifieth the gold? And, "Whosoever shall swear by the altar, it is nothing; but whosoever sweareth by the gift that is upon it, he is guilty." Ye fools and blind: for whether is greater, the gift, or the altar that sanctifieth the gift? Whoso therefore shall swear by the altar, sweareth by it, and by all things thereon. And whoso shall swear by the temple, sweareth by it, and by him that dwelleth therein. And he that shall swear by heaven, sweareth by the throne of God, and by him that sitteth thereon.

" 'Woe unto you, scribes and Pharisees, hypocrites! For ye pay tithe of mint and anise and cummin, and have omitted the weightier matters of the law, judgment, mercy, and faith: these ought ye to have done, and not to leave the other undone. Ye blind guides, which strain at a gnat, and swallow a camel.

" 'Woe unto you, scribes and Pharisees, hypocrites! For ye make clean the outside of the cup and of the platter, but within they are full of extortion and excess. Thou blind Pharisee, cleanse first that which is within the cup and platter, that the outside of them may be clean also.

" 'Woe unto you, scribes and Pharisees, hypocrites! For ye are like unto whited sepulchres, which indeed appear beautiful outward, but are within full of dead men's bones, and of all uncleanness. Even so ye also outwardly appear righteous unto men, but within ye are full of hypocrisy and iniquity.

" 'Woe unto you, scribes and Pharisees, hypocrites! Because ye build the tombs of the prophets, and garnish the sepulchres of the righteous, and say, If we had been in the days of our fathers, we would not have been partakers with them in the blood of the prophets.

" 'Wherefore ye be witnesses unto yourselves, that ye are the children of them which killed the prophets. Fill ye up then the measure of your fathers. Ye serpents, ye generation of vipers, how can ye escape the damnation of hell? Wherefore, behold, I send unto you prophets, and wise men, and scribes: and some of them ye shall kill and crucify; and some of them shall ye scourge in your synagogues, and persecute them from city to city: that upon you may come all the righteous blood shed upon the earth, from the blood of righteous Abel unto the blood of Zacharias son of Barachias, whom ye slew between the temple and the altar. Verily I say unto you, "All these things shall come upon this generation."

" 'O! Jerusalem, Jerusalem, thou that killest the prophets, and stonest them which are sent unto thee, how often would I have gathered thy children together, even as a hen gathereth her chickens under her wings, and ye would not! Behold, your house is left unto you desolate. For I say unto you, ye shall not see Me henceforth, till ye shall say, "Blessed is he that cometh in the name of the Lord." ' "

The elders and the chief priests and the scribes beat their staves upon the tiled stones in their exasperation and called for the first of many to bare false witnesses against Him, whom saith, "I heard His disciples sayeth, 'Let Mary who was possessed of demons goeth away from us for women are not worthy of life.' And He saith, 'Lo, I will draweth her so I wilt make her a man so that she too may becomest a living spirit which is like you men; for every woman who maketh herself a man wilt entereth into the kingdom of heaven.' "

And a second of the deceptive witnesses presented himself, for the Pharisees knoweth the Law of Moses Lawgiver that one witness shall not rise up against a man for any iniquity, or for any sin, in any sin that he sinneth: at the mouth of two witnesses, or at the mouth of three witnesses, shall the matter be established. The second false witness saith, "I heard this He saith, 'He who shalt not hate his own father and mother cannot be mine disciple. And he who shalt not hate his brothers and sisters cannot carry his cross as I have, and is not worthy of Me.' "

And a spurious friend from His childhood saith, "Now when He was five years old there was a great rain upon the earth, and the Child walked about therein. And the rain was very terrible: and He gathered the water together into a pool and commanded with a word that it should become clear: and forthwith it did so. Again, He took of the clay which came of that pool and made thereof to the number of twelve sparrows. Now it was the sabbath day when He did this among the children of the Hebrews: and the children of the Hebrews went and said unto Joseph His father: 'Lo, thy Son was playing with us and He took clay and made sparrows which it was not right to do upon the sabbath, and He hath broken it.' And Joseph went to the Child , and said unto Him: 'Wherefore hast thou done this which it was not right to do on the sabbath?' But He spread forth (opened) His hands and commanded the sparrows, saying: 'Go forth into the height and fly: ye shall not meet death at any man's hands.' And they flew and began to cry out and praise almighty God!' "

And another forged friend from **His** childhood saith, "Yea! Yea! I witnessed it. Now on another day, when **He** climbed up upon a house with the children, **He** began to play with them: but one of the boys fell down through the door out of the upper chamber and died straightway. And when the children saw it they fled all of them, but **He** remained alone in the house. And when the parents of the child which had died came they spake against **Him** saying: 'Of a truth thou madest him fall.' But **He** said: '**I never made him fall!**': nevertheless they accused him still. **He** therefore came down from the house and stood over the dead child and cried with a loud voice, calling him by his name: '**Zeno, Zeno, arise and say if I made thee fall'.** And on a sudden he arose and said: "Nay, **Lord**." And when his parents saw this great miracle which **He** did, they glorified **God**, and worshipped **Him**!"

And the high priest stood up in the midst, and asked **Jesus**, saying, "Answerest **Thou** nothing? What is it which these witness against **Thee**?" But **He** held **His** peace, and answered nothing. He knoweth if a soul sin, and hear the voice of swearing, and is a witness, whether he hath seen or known of it; if he do not utter it, then he shall bear his iniquity, but if there is no sin in the soul and he utters not, shall he bear iniquity?

And Saul of Tarsus saith, "For we are the circumcision on the eighth day, of the stock of Israel, of the tribe of Benjamin, an Hebrew of the Hebrews; as touching the law, a Pharisee, which worship **God** in the spirit, and reject in **Christ Jesus**, whom is not the only begotten **Son** of the **LORD God** of Israel. All that believeth in **Him** shall perish, and be condemned. Men and brethren, I am a Pharisee, the son of a Pharisee: of the hope and concerning the resurrection of the dead is **Jesus of Nazareth of the Galilee** called into question!

Then Saul calleth into question the fulfilment of Prophecies foretelling the coming of the Messiah in the Nazarene, "**Jesus of Nazareth of the Galilee**, **Ye** have quoted the prophet, '**All ye shall be offended because of Me this night: for it is written, I will smite the shepherd, and the sheep of the flock shall be scattered abroad.**' And it shall come to pass in that day, that the prophets shall be ashamed every one of his vision, when he hath prophesied; neither shall they wear a rough garment to deceive."

Nicodemus holdeth not his tongue, "Ye daub the truth. Shalt **He** proclaim the **Word**? 'O! sword, against my shepherd, and against the man that is my fellow.' **He** is no prophet, **He** is an husbandman; for man taught **Him** to keep cattle from **His** youth. And one shall say unto **Him**, 'What are these wounds in thine hands?' Then **He** shall answer, '**Those with which I was wounded in the house of My friends.**' "

Saul saith, "Zebud spake, 'also the Strength of Israel will not lie nor repent: for he is not a man, that he should repent.' Hath **Ye** risen against Rome and overthrown the eagle? Shuld ye not judge among the nations, and should ye not rebuke many people? And they shall beat their swords into plowshares, and their spears into pruninghooks: nation shall not lift up sword against nation, neither shall they learn war any more. Hath we mistaken Rome's oppression for peace? The **Messiah** is Prophesied to spread the **Word** of **God**. When the **LORD** shalt be king of all creation and the gods of foreign lands damned to the dead. One day shalt be one **LORD** and **His** name one!"

"Teacher, ye speak in circles," Nicodemus pleadeth, "We hath heard these arguments. Relent! Repent thy words against this **Rabbi**?"

Saul in his seething anger saith, "Hath this Jesus of Nazareth of the Galilee heard of my arguments against Him? Is this Jesus of God omnipotent? Omniscient? Omnipresent? Bah! Fie! Shalt Ye set up an ensign for the nations? As propecied by Isaiah! And shalt Ye assemble the outcasts of Israel? And gather together the dispersed of Judah from the four corners of the earth?

"Isaiah saith, 'It shall come to pass in that day, that the LORD shall beat off from the channel of the river unto the stream of Egypt, and ye shall be gathered one by one, O! ye children of Israel. And it shall come to pass in that day, that the great trumpet shall be blown, and they shall come which were ready to perish in the land of Assyria, and the outcasts in the land of Egypt, and shall worship the LORD in the holy mount at Jerusalem.'

"Jesus, Thou art not the Messiah foretold. We are squandered, scattered people. Thy lies are most bold! When Israel was a child, then the LORD loved him, and called the LORD's son out of Egypt! We Israel, art the sons of God, not Thee!"

And the LORD hardened the heart of Pharisees, and they hearkened not unto Him, and He willingly gave His back to the smiters, and His cheeks to them that plucked off the hair: He hid not His face from shame and spitting, for they abhor Him, they flee far from Him, and spare not to spit in His face. And they became possessed in their spirit to spit in His face, and to buffet Him; and others to smote Him with the palms of their hands, and whilst the Pharisees thought on this, then Saul did. ✠

Chapter 4
"The Conversation of the Conversion"

HEN SAUL, WHO WOULD FROM four years hence be counted amongst **His** Apostles, spat in **His** face, and buffeted **Him**; and smote **Him** with the palms of his hands; the clapping of Saul's palms against **His** cheeks, both **His** first and **His** other offered cheek, dinned throughout the echoing chamber. **His** collapsed nose bled and **His** blackened eyes swoln, blindfolding **Him** of **His** own flesh and **His** own blood so **He** saw not the smoting hand, nor whom saith unto **Him**, "**Messiah**? Fie! Prophecy unto us, **Christ**! Whatever is the name of he who smote **Thee**?" And **He** saith, **"Saul, Saul, why persecutest thou Me?** And Saul answereth not for his body trembled and his soul was astonished.

And **He** did Prophecy unto the Pharisee concerning the coming acts of the Apostles, and there was a distant echo of Saul's own voice coming from **His** mouth:

"Thou art verily a man which is a Jew, born in Tarsus, a city in Cilicia, yet brought up in the Holy City at the feet of Gamaliel, and taught according to the perfect manner of the law of the fathers, and art zealous toward God, as My disciples all are this day. And thou persecutes this Way unto the death, binding and delivering into prisons both men and women: as when the Jews crieth out with a loud voice, and stop their ears so they heareth not the truth of My martyred Stephen:

" 'Ye stiffnecked and uncircumcised in heart and ears, ye do always resist the Holy Ghost: as your fathers did, so do ye. Which of the prophets have not your fathers persecuted? and they have slain them which shewed before of the coming of the Just One; of whom ye have been now the betrayers and murderers: who have received the law by the disposition of angels, and have not kept it.' But he, being full of the Holy Ghost, looked up stedfastly into heaven, and saw the glory of God, and Me standing on the right hand of God, and said, 'Behold, I see the heavens opened, and the Son of man standing on the right hand of God.'

"When they heard these things, they were cut to the heart, and they gnashed on him with their teeth. And run upon My martyred Stephen with one accord, and cast him out of the city, and stone him as My Father decreed, 'Bring forth him that hath cursed without the camp; and let all that heard him lay their hands upon his head, and let all the congregation stone him.' And the witnesses lay down their clothes at thy feet while they stone My martyred Stephen, whom calls upon My Father, and saying, 'Lord Jesus, into Thine hand I commit My spirit: Thou hast redeemed Me, O! LORD God of truth.' And he

kneels down, and cries with a loud voice, 'Lord, lay not this sin to their charge.' And when My martyred Stephen says this, he falls asleep. And thou consents unto his death.

"At this time there is a great persecution against My church which is at Jerusalem; and they are all scattered abroad throughout the regions of Judaea and Samaria, except the apostles. As for thee, thou maketh havock of the church, entering into every house, and haling men and women committing them to prison.

"As also the high priest doth bear thee witness, and all the estate of the elders: from whom also I received letters unto the brethren, and goeth to Damascus, to bring them which were there bound unto Jerusalem, for to be punished. As thou made thy journey, and was come nigh unto Damascus about noon, suddenly there shines from heaven a great light, above the brightness of the sun, round about thee. And thou falls unto the ground, and heard a voice saying unto thee:

"'Saul, Saul, why persecutest thou Me?' And thou answereth, 'Who art Thou, Lord'? And I say unto thee, 'I AM Jesus of Nazareth of the Galilee, whom thou persecutest.' And they that are with thee saw indeed the light, and art afraid and stand speechless, hearing a voice, but seeing no man.

"And trembling and astonished thou saith, 'Lord, what wilt Thou have Me to do?' And I say unto thee, 'Arise, and go into Damascus; and there it shall be told thee of all things which are appointed for thee to do.' And when thou can not see for the glory of that light, being led by the hand of them that are with thee, thou come into Damascus.

He prophesies the stoning of His martyred Stephen whilst clothes lay at the feet of Saul!

"And thou art three days without sight, and neither did eat nor drink. And there was a certain disciple at Damascus, named Ananias. And to him I say in a vision, 'Ananias. Arise, and go into the street which is called Straight, and enquire in the house of Judas for one called Saul, of Tarsus: for, behold, he prayeth, and hath seen in a vision a man named Ananias coming in, and putting his hand on him, that he might receive his sight.'

"Then Ananias answer unto Me, 'Lord, I have heard by many of this man, how much evil he hath done to thy saints at Jerusalem: and here he hath authority from the chief priests to bind all that call on thy name.'

"But I say unto him, 'Go thy way: for he is a chosen vessel unto Me, to bear My name before the Gentiles, and kings, and the children of Israel: for I will shew him how great things he must suffer for My name's sake.'

"And Ananias, a devout man according to the law, having a good report of all the Jews which dwelt there, comes unto thee, and stands, and says unto thee, 'Brother Saul, receive thy sight.' And the same hour thou looks up upon him. And he said, 'The God of our fathers hath chosen thee, that thou shouldest know His will, and see that Just One, and shouldest hear the voice of His mouth. For thou shalt be His witness unto all men of what thou hast seen and heard. And now why tarriest thou? arise, and be baptized, and wash away thy sins, calling on the name of the Lord.' And immediately there fall from thy eyes as it had been scales: and thou shalt receiveth sight forthwith, and arise, and be baptized.

And when thou hath received meat, thou art strengthened. Then art thou certain days with the dis-

---

He *prophesies Saul's conversion into Paul the Apostle on the road to Damascus!*

ciples which were at Damascus. And straightway thou preacheth Christ in the synagogues, that I AM the Son of God. Thou art not disobedient unto the heavenly vision: but shewed first unto them of Damascus, and at Jerusalem, and throughout all the coasts of Judaea, and then to the Gentiles, that they should repent and turn to God, and do works meet for repentance. For these causes the Jews caught thee in the temple, and went about to kill thee. Having therefore obtained help of God witnessing both to small and great, saying none other things than those which the prophets and Moses did say should come: that I should suffer, and that I should be the first that should rise from the dead, and should shew light unto the people, and to the Gentiles.

"But all that heareth thou art be amazed, and saith; 'Is not this he that destroyed them which called on this name in Jerusalem, and came hither for that intent, that he might bring them bound unto the chief priests?' But thou art increased the more in strength, and confounded the Jews which dwelt at Damascus, proving that this is very Christ!

"And thy brethren taketh counsel to kill thee: but their laying await is known of thee. And they watch the gates day and night to kill thee. Then the disciples taketh thee by night, and let thee down by the wall in a basket.

"And when thou cometh to Jerusalem, thou assayeth to join thyself to My disciples: but they art all afraid of thee, and believe not that thou art a disciple, for thou breathed out threatenings and slaughter against My disciples and standeth by with clothes at thy feet when My martyred Stephen is stoned.

"Howbeit it then they saw Me saying unto thee,

'Make haste, and get thee quickly out of Jerusalem: for they will not receive thy testimony concerning me.' And thou says, 'Lord, they know that I imprisoned and beat in every synagogue them that believed on thee: and when the blood of thy martyr Stephen was shed, I also was standing by, and consenting unto his death, and kept the raiment of them that slew him.' And I say unto thee, 'Depart: for I will send thee far hence unto the Gentiles.'

Ignoring the woeful and wonderful prophecy that tore the soul of Saul of Taurus in twain, the high priest arose, and Caiaphas said unto Him, "Answerest Thou nothing? What is it which these witness against Thee?" But He held His peace, And the high priest answered and said unto Him, "I adjure thee by the living God, that Thou tell us whether Thou be the Christ, the Son of God."

He saith unto him, "Thou hast said: nevertheless I say unto you, Hereafter shall ye see the Son of man sitting on the right hand of power, and coming in the clouds of heaven." The idols of Egypt shall be moved at His presence, and the heart of Egypt shall melt in the midst of it. And He will set the Egyptians against the Egyptians: and they shall fight every one against his brother, and every one against his neighbour; city against city, and kingdom against kingdom. As will His will be upon Israel!

"Answereth the question posed," Caiaphas demanded, ""I adjure thee by the living God, that Thou tell us whether Thou be the Christ, the Son of God."

"I AM!"

"Fraud! I striketh Thee with Aaron's rod!" Then the high priest rent his clothes, saying, "He hath spoken blasphemy; what further need have we of witnesses? Behold, now ye have heard His blasphemy. He that blasphemeth the name of the LORD, He shall surely be put to death, and all the congregation shall certainly stone Him: as well the stranger, as He that is born in the land, when He blasphemeth the name of the LORD, shall be put to death!"

Then did they spit in His face, and buffeted Him; and others smote Him with the palms of their hands. When they smote Him on His right cheek, He turned to them the other also. And the elders, chief priests, and scribes who smote Him remembereth their spies reporteth that He had taught a lesson, "Ye have heard that it hath been said, 'An eye for an eye, and a tooth for a tooth.' But I say unto you, that ye resist not evil: but whosoever shall smite thee on thy right cheek, turn to him the other also." For a Jew is wont to striketh a man with the backs of their hands. And then the elders, chief priests, and scribes in their arrogance they turned their hands to smote Him with the backs of their hands.

And as Saul spit in His face, and buffeted Him, and smote Him with the palm and back of his right hand, he curseth, "Answer me! How can God the Father be also the Son and the Holy Ghost? I tell you, God is One! The LORD himself spake, 'I am the LORD, and there is none else, there is no God beside Me: I girded thee, though thou hast not known Me: I am the first, and I am the last; and beside Me there is no God.' God is the LORD and there is no other. Ye are a false prophet and a false prophet is

---

Caiaphas demands to know if He is the Son of God, to which "I AM!" and Saul of Tarsus, whom persecuteth Him, smote Him on His cheek!

but Satan's brother! There can never be a Holy Trinity! **Jesus**! The **Son of God**? 'Tis but madness!"

Then it came to pass that the soldiers leadeth **Him** from the House of Caiaphas onto the porch and they spit in **His** face, and buffeted **Him**, and smote **Him** with the fists of their hands and the whips of cords.

And Saul of Tarsus saw the multitudes on the porch of the House of Caiaphas, those most loyal to the elders, the chief priests, and the scribes, whom were the chaff **He** will burn up with unquenchable fire when in **His** hand is a fan.

Nary any of those of the very great multitude that went before, and that followed, and hath spread their garments in the way; others cut down branches from the trees, and strawed them in the way, saying, "Hosanna to the son of David: Blessed is **He** that cometh in the name of the **LORD**; Hosanna in the highest" stood on the porch of the house of Caiaphas. These are the wheat that **He** shalt gather into the garner, when **He** will thoroughly purge **His** floor.

And this most loyal of multitudes, the sycophants, and schemers whom desired to be nearest power and not the Truth, saith, "Did not Isaiah foretell the coming of this **Jesus of Nazareth of the Galilee**?" Their mockery and scorn assaulted **Him**. "O! Wherefore art **Thou** the **Messiah**? Wherethrough **God** ye cometh to Israel: The children of Isaac, never to Ishmael! Witherward salvation, shalt we followeth **Thy** lead? **Messiah**! **Messiah**! I adjure **Thee** by the living **God**, that **Thou** tell us whether **Thou** be the **Christ**, the **Son of God**! Whencesoever shalt our sins by **Him** be released? What thinkest ye of the **Messiah**! O! Saul the Pharisee, son of a Pharisee?"

And Saul of Tarsus the Pharisee, the son of a Pharisee, saith, "There riseth up among you a **prophet**, or a **dreamer** of dreams, and giveth thee a sign or a wonder, And the sign or the wonder come to pass, whereof he spake unto thee, saying, 'Let us go after other gods, which thou hast not known, and let us serve them'; thou shalt not hearken unto the words of that prophet, or that dreamer of dreams: for the LORD your God proveth you, to know whether ye love the LORD your God with all your heart and with all your soul. Ye shall walk after the LORD your God, and fear Him, and keep His commandments, and obey His voice, and ye shall serve Him, and cleave unto Him.

"And that prophet, or that dreamer of dreams, shall be put to death; because He hath spoken to turn you away from the LORD your God, which brought you out of the land of Egypt, and redeemed you out of the house of bondage, to thrust thee out of the way which the LORD thy God commanded thee to walk in. So shalt thou put the evil away from the midst of thee. If thy brother, the son of thy mother, or thy son, or thy daughter, or the wife of thy bosom, or thy friend, which is as thine own soul, entice thee secretly, saying, 'Let us go and serve other gods', which thou hast not known, thou, nor thy fathers; namely, of the gods of the people which are round about you, nigh unto thee, or far off from thee, from the one end of the earth even unto the other end of the earth; thou shalt not consent unto Him, nor hearken unto Him; neither shall thine eye pity Him, neither shalt thou spare, neither shalt thou conceal Him: But thou shalt surely kill Him; thine hand shall be first upon Him to put Him to death, and afterwards the hand of all the people."

Chapter 5
"Denied Thrice and the Potter's Price"

**HEREAT SIMON PETER FOL-**lowed **Him**, and so did another disciple: that disciple known unto the high priest, and went in with **Him** into the palace of the high priest. But Peter stood at the door without. Then went out that other disciple, which was known unto the high priest, and spake unto her that kept the door, and brought in Peter. Then saith the damsel that kept the door unto Peter, "And thou, also wast with **Jesus of Nazareth of the Galilee**?" He saith, "I knowest not, neither understand I what thou sayeth."

And the maid, with the voice of doves, tabering upon her breasts, saith, "Surely thou art one of them for thou art a Galilean and thy speech agreeth thereto." He saith, "Nay! faith. I am not."

*Peter denies his **Christ** thrice before the cock crows once!*

And the servants and officers stood there, who had made a fire of coals; for it was cold: and they warmed themselves: and Peter stood with them, and warmed himself. And Simon Peter stood and warmed himself. They said therefore unto him, "Art not thou also one of His disciples?" He denied it, and said, "I am not."

One of the servants of the high priest, being his kinsman whose ear Peter cut off, saith, "Did not I see thee in the garden with Him? Yea! ye hath cut off my kinsman's ear! He is a disciple of the criminal Jesus! Crucify him in turn!"

And Peter then denied again, "A murrain on thy words. I doth not know this Man of whom you speak. God shalt mend my soul if I lieth. God warrant me! I am not one with Him. A devil's name! bear not false witness against me. I am not nor ever hath been this Man's disciple!"

And immediately the cock crew. And then He turned, and looked upon Peter from the porch of the house of Caiaphas. And Peter remembered His words, how He had said unto him, **"Before the cock crow, thou shalt deny Me thrice."** Heretherefore Peter remembereth the Prophecy of His Lord and Saviour, whenat Peter hath answered and said unto Him, "Though all men shall be offended because of Thee, yet will I never be offended!" and He said unto him, **"Verily I say unto thee, that this night, before the cock crow, thou shalt deny Me thrice,"** and Peter said unto Him, "Though I should die with Thee, yet will I not deny Thee."

And he wept bitterly and prayed a prayer of David, "Have mercy upon me, O! God, according to Thy lovingkindness: according unto the multitude of Thy tender mercies blot out my transgressions. Wash me throughly from mine iniquity, and cleanse me from my sin. For I acknowledge my transgressions: and my sin is ever before me.

Against Thee, Thee only, have I sinned, and done this evil in Thy sight: that Thou mightest be justified when Thou speakest, and be clear when Thou judgest. Behold, I was shapen in iniquity; and in sin did my mother conceive me. Behold, Thou desirest truth in the inward parts: and in the hidden part Thou shalt make me to know wisdom. Purge me with hyssop, and I shall be clean: wash me, and I shall be whiter than snow. Make me to hear joy and gladness; that the bones which thou hast broken may rejoice. Hide thy face from my sins, and blot out all mine iniquities. Create in me a clean heart, O! God; and renew a right spirit within me. Cast me not away from thy presence; and take not Thy Holy Ghost from me. Restore unto me the joy of Thy salvation; and uphold me with Thy free spirit. Then will I teach transgressors Thy ways; and sinners shall be converted unto Thee. Deliver me from bloodguiltiness, O! God, Thou God of my salvation: and my tongue shall sing aloud of Thy righteousness. O! LORD, open Thou my lips; and my mouth shall shew forth Thy praise. For Thou desirest not sacrifice; else would I give it: Thou delightest not in burnt offering. The sacrifices of God are a broken spirit: a broken and a contrite heart, O! God, Thou wilt not despise. Do good in thy good pleasure unto Zion: build thou the walls of Jerusalem. Then shalt Thou be pleased with the sacrifices of righteousness, with burnt offering and whole burnt offering: then shall they offer bullocks upon thine altar."

And as soon as it was day, the elders of the people and the chief priests and the scribes came together, and led Him from their council, saying, "Art thou the Christ? tell us." And He said unto them, "If I tell you, ye will not believe: and if I also ask you, ye will not answer Me, nor let Me go. Hereafter shall the Son of man sit on the right hand of the power of God."

And said they all, "Art thou then the **Son of God**?" And **He** said unto them, **"Ye say that I AM."** And they said, "What need we any further witness? for we ourselves have heard of **His** own mouth."

When the morning came, all the chief priests and elders of the people took counsel against **Him** to put **Him** to death: And when they had bound **Him**, they led **Him** away, and delivered **Him** to Pontius Pilate, the governor.

Then Judas, which had betrayed **Him**, when he saw that the elders and the chief priests and the scribes condemned **Him**, repented himself, and brought again the thirty pieces of silver to the chief priests and elders, saying, "I have sinned in that I have betrayed the innocent blood." For the elders and the chief priests and the scribes, even Judas, knoweth if the ox gores a male or female slave, he must give thirty shekels of silver to the slave's master, and the ox must be stoned. The **LORD** writteth poetic punishments and apt agonies into the thirty pieces of silver.

And they said, "What is that to us? see thou to that." Then in anger he cast down the pieces of silver in the temple, and departed, and went in the garden, whereat he had betrayed **Him** with a kiss. He lashed a rope to the strongest bough of a tree and hanged himself. His neck broke not as he flung himself down and he convulsed and strained under the wrenching and strangling of the rope. He clutched and clawed at his neck, his face scratched to the very bone, the

Judas hangs himself in the garden called Gethsemene where he betrayed **Him***!*

flesh of his cheeks hung in ribbons of flesh and his blood cascaded down his chest and back.

Then an aged man appeared walking through the garden known as Gethsemane, and he looked upon Judas and saith, "Art thou a disciple of His? Were you not also with Him? Of a truth this fellow also was with Him: for he is a Galileaean." And Judas denied not, gasping and straining to speak, "I am."

"Why?" enquired the aged man, "And did thee not, one of the twelve, go unto the chief priests, to betray Him unto them; and when they heard it, they were glad, and promised to give thee money? And thou sought how thou might conveniently betray Him?" And Judas denied not, "I did."

"Why? the aged man continued, "Did not God so love the world, that he gave His only begotten Son, that whosoever believeth in Him should not perish, but have everlasting life? Did not God send His Son into the world to condemn the world; but that the world through Him might be saved? Is he that believeth on Him not condemned: but he that believeth not is condemned already, because he hath not believed in the name of the only begotten Son of God?" And Judas denied not, "Yes, God so loved."

"Why? Why?" enquired the aged man, "Because thou was with Him six days before the passover and came to Bethany, where Lazarus was, which had been dead, whom He raised from the dead. There they made Him a supper; and Martha served: but Lazarus was one of them that sat at the table with Him. Then took Mary a pound of ointment of spikenard, very costly, and anointed His feet, and wiped His feet with her hair: and the house filled with the odour of the ointment. Was there not some indignation within

Judas rebukes Mary for wasting expensive ointment and the seed of his betrayal is planted!

His disciples, and thou saith, "Why was this waste of the ointment made?" For the spikenard might have been sold for more than three hundred pence, and have been given to the poor. Didst not thou and thy fellows murmured against her?" And Judas denied not, "We did."

"Did not **He** saith, **'Let her alone; why trouble ye her? she hath wrought a good work on Me. For ye have the poor with you always, and whensoever ye will ye may do them good: but Me ye have not always. She hath done what she could: she is come aforehand to anoint My body to the burying. Verily I say unto you, 'Wheresoever this gospel shall be preached throughout the whole world, this also that she hath done shall be spoken of for a memorial of her.'** " And Judas denied not, "**He** did."

"And did not thee, one of the twelve, go unto the chief priests, to betray **Him** unto them; and when they heard it, they were glad, and promised to give thou money. And though sought how he might conveniently betray **Him**?" And Judas denied not, "Verily, verily, I did."

And the bough of the tree broke and Judas did fall headlong. Looking around for the aged man, Judas saw him not. And knowing he spoke to that old serpent, called the Devil, and Satan, took he did his dagger from his sash and he cut upon his gut. He winced and cried out, digging into his own innards. The physical pain of his mortal flesh, though excruciating, was but a splinter to the spiritual pain, the flaying of his immortal soul in the betraying of the **Son of God**. He pulled forth his innards and his bowels gushed out and verily a mangy mongrel feasted upon his viscera and lapped his blood, her pups yipping and tugging on a length of his innards, growling and quarrelling over the choicest scraps of his flesh.

And the chief priests picked the silver pieces off of the

cobbled-stones, and said, "It is not lawful for to put them into the treasury, because it is the price of blood." And they took counsel, and bought with them the potter's field, to bury strangers in. Wherefore that field was called, the field of blood, unto this day. Then was fulfilled that which was spoken by Jeremy the prophet, saying, "And they took the thirty pieces of silver, the price of **Him** that was valued, whom they of the children of Israel did value; and gave them for the potter's field, as the **LORD** appointed me."

When the morning was come, all the chief priests and elders of the people took counsel against Jesus to put him to death: And when they had bound him, they led him away, from the House of Caiaphas and delivered him to Pontius Pilate the governor, in the the hall of judgment. For **He** hath heard the slander of many: fear was on every side: while they took counsel together against **Him**, they devised to take away **His** life. And they themselves went not into the Praetorium, the governor's house, lest they should be defiled; but that they might eat the passover. Pilate then went out unto them, and said, "What accusation bring ye against this **Man**?"

They answered and said unto him, "If **He** were not a malefactor, we would not have delivered **Him** up unto thee, O! Pontius Pilate, Prefector!"

Then said Pilate unto them, "Take ye **Him**, and judge **Him** according to your law." The Jews counted amongst the Chaff therefore said unto him, "It is not lawful for us to put any man to death" that the saying of Jesus might be fulfilled, which He spake, signifying what death He should die.

Then Pilate entered into the Praetorium again, and called Him, and said unto Him, "Art thou the King of the Jews?" He answered him, **"Sayest thou this thing of thyself, or did others tell it thee of Me?"**

Pilate answered, "Am I a Jew? Thine own nation and the chief priests have delivered Thee unto me: what hast Thou done?" He answered, **"My kingdom is not of this world: if My kingdom were of this world, then would My servants fight, that I should not be delivered to the Jews: but now is My kingdom not from hence."**

Pilate therefore said unto Him, "Art Thou a king then?" And Saul of Tarsus, who defiled himself to enter the Praetorium, interjected, "We found this fellow perverting the nation, and forbidding to give tribute to Caesar, saying that He Himself is Christ a King." He answered, **"All thou sayest that I am a king. To this end was I born, and for this cause came I into the world, that I should bear witness unto the truth. Every one that is of the truth heareth My voice."**

Pilate saith unto Him, "What is truth?" And He answereth not. And Pilate saith unto Saul, "Saul, from Tarsus, the Pharisee, the son of a Pharisee, circumcised the eighth day, of the stock of Israel, of the tribe of Benjamin, an Hebrew of the Hebrews; as touching the law, a Pharisee, speaketh thee thy charges against this Jew."

And Saul saith, "We found this fellow perverting the nation. He is guilty of the crimes against Rome of sedition!"

"List the charges arraigned against this man."

A Roman Mongrel proudly, boastfully, took his place

The elders, chief priests, and scribes accuse Him of sedition before Pontius Pilate!

and saith, "The chief priests of the Sanhedrin charge this **Rabbi** of their own faith with conspiring with demons during exorcisms. Healing lazars (that is to say lepers), those cursed souls condemned by the gods to suffer sins of a past life in this life, with sorcery and with this same sorcery, he raiseth the dead from Hades. **He** claimeth to be the **Son of God** and a King of a heavenly kingdom."

And Pilate saith and asketh of **Him**, "Caesar rules as king of Judah; I am his Prefect. Wherefore art **Thy** kingdom, **Thy** highness?"

But **He** held **His** peace.

"Doth **Thee** answer not-a-thing. Hearest **Thou** not how many things they witness against **Thee**?" Pilate demanded.

And Saul protested, "**He** stirreth up against Rome the jewry, this **Jesus of Nazareth of the Galilee**."

And Pilate, seeking to wash his hands of this **Jesus of Nazareth of the Galilee**, saith, "Sayeth thou 'Galilee'? Whether be it this man of Galilee? This **King of the Jews** is not of my jurisdiction. Let Herod, who is rendered by Tiberius the King of the Jews. Let him render his verdict."

And when Herod Antipas saw **Him**, he was exceeding glad: for he was desirous to see **Him** of a long season, because he had heard many things of **Him**; and he hoped to have seen some miracle done by **Him**. Then he questioned with **Him** in many words: "Desirous for many a season hath I been to see **Thee**, **Jesus of Nazareth of the Galilee**. Ex-

ceeding glad am I. Hath I heard many things of **Thee**.
I hope to see many miracles done by **Thee**. I heareth
Thee keepeth company with lepers. Doth **Thee** heal the
lepers of their manhood whenst it shrivels on the branch
and falleth off like autumn leaves? Doth **Thee** pick from
the dirt their withered worm and restore it? Come now,
healer, giveth back unto my eunuch his virility. Touch
him wherein he wast untimely pruned of the bush. Sprunt
from his lacking seed a great, stout, erect oak. Heal him.
Maketh him a man.

"Nay?

"I heareth **Thee** keepeth company with prostitutes.
Art these harlots **Thy** harem, **Thy** concubines? If **Thee** art
the **King of the Jews**, where art **Thy** queen to swell big bel-
lied at the strike of **Thy** serpent? Whereat art **Thy** heirs to
propagate **Thy** dynasty. Is not one of **Thy** disciples a woman? Is she beloved of **Thee**? I heareth **Thee** kisseth her on the
lips? Bring forth Mary of Magdala. There shalt be on this
day a royal wedding. Hurrah! Hurrah! Sendeth the heralds
to trumpet the news of the marriage of the King of the Jews.
Marry her and maketh her **Thy** queen. I shalt giveth **Thee**
my kingdom. Let her giveth **Thee** many sons to render unto
David an heir to his house!"

But **He** answered him nothing.

"Nay, faith," Herod Antipas saith full of boredom and
disgust, "I grow weary of this game. Convey the **King of the
Jews** back to Pontius Pilate. What sort of sport is **He**? Fie!
on **Thee**. King of the Jews! Fie!"

Now at that feast Pilate, as was his custom, released unto them one prisoner, whomsoever they desired. And there was one named Jesus Bar-Abba, which lay bound with them that had made insurrection with him, who had committed murder in the insurrection. And the multitude crying aloud began to desire him to do as he had ever done unto them.

And Pilate, when he had called together the chief priests and the rulers and the people, whom were the chaff **He** will burn up with unquenchable fire when in **His** hand is a fan.

Nary any of those of the very great multitude that went before, and that followed, and hath spread their garments in the way; others cut down branches from the trees, and strawed them in the way, saying, "Hosanna to the son of David: Blessed is **He** that cometh in the name of the **LORD**; Hosanna in the highest" stood on the porch of the house of Caiaphas. These are the wheat that **He** shalt gather into the garner, when **He** will thoroughly purge **His** floor.

Pontius Pilate said unto the Chaff, "Ye hath brought this man unto me, as one that perverteth the people and behold, I, having examined **Him** before you, have found no fault in this **Man**, touching those things whereof ye accuse **Him**: No, nor yet Herod, for I sent **Thee** to him; and no, nothing worthy of death is done by **Him**. I will therefore chastise **Him**, and release **Him**."

And Saul stood amidst the Chaff and saith in profane poetry, "**His** blasphemy, the Word justifies **Him**! **He** the Messiah is not. Deny **Him**! The **False Prophet** standeth ye not by **Him**."And a few of the Chaff saith, "We deny **Him** O! **LORD**. Crucify **Him**. We standeth not by **Him**. Crucify **Him**!"

And Pontius Pilate protested, "Why, what evil hath

He done?"

And Saul proudly saith, "Speaking our truths, we cannot belie Him! He the Messiah is not. Decry Him. Of His evils, ye must ye descry Him!" And more of the Chaff saith, "We decry Him O! LORD. Crucify Him. Descry Him. Yea faith! Crucify Him!"

And Pilate saith, "I canst not find any crime against Him."

And Saul boastfully saith, "The murderous Apostles ally Him! He the Messiah is not. Defy Him. Taketh ye pains ye not deify Him!" And many more of the Chaff saith, "We defy Him O! LORD. Crucify Him! Deify Him? Nay faith. Crucify Him!"

And Pilate wearily and rejectedly saith, "I have found no cause of death in Him: I will therefore chastise Him, and let Him go. Taketh this 'King of the Jews' and haveth Him thus scourged."

And a Centurion amidst the crowd stepped forward and pleadeth unto Pontius Pilate, "Prefect, mayest I offer testimony. Whenst He entered into Capernaum, there came unto Him, I, a centurion, beseeching Him, and saying, 'LORD, my servant lieth at home sick of the palsy, grievously tormented.' And He saith unto me that He will come and heal him. And I knoweth I am not worthy that He shouldest come under my roof: but He speak the word only, and my servant shall be healed. For I am a man under heathen authority, having soldiers under me: who goeth when I say 'go; who come and when I say 'come', and my servants doeth this when I say, 'do this.' When He heard He said of me a heathen and a Centurion, 'Verily, I have not found so great faith, no, not in Israel. That many shall come from the east and west, and shall sit down with Abraham, and Isaac, and Jacob, in the kingdom of heaven. But the children of the kingdom shall be cast out into outer darkness: there shall be weeping and gnashing of teeth.' And He said unto me the heathen and the Centurion, 'Go thy way; and as thou hast believed, so be it done unto thee.' And He healed my servant in the selfsame hour. Punish this man not, my liege."

Exasperated at the Jews, Pilate expunged Him of their accusations, "Scourge the King of the Jews. Purge me of His subjects."

Chapter 6
"The Suffering of the Servent"

THE CRIMINAL CHARGED WITH sedition against Rome and Israel was soon to be lashed with ropes to the iron rings of a pillar removed from the court of Pontius Pilate reserved for such unseemly work. The executioners, those Roman Mongrels, whom delight in infliction of pain, suffering, and agony, stood armed with rods of wood, whips made of cords and ropes of unnatural implements.

The Roman Mongrels, bereft of all the gifts and graces given by **God** to the races of men, were filthy mongrels with rough hewed hands cracked from the hardest of labours required of criminals condemned and the lone son of a Senator's family chastised to serve as an executioner for insubordination and desertion, due to his high birth his superiors spared him from *fustuarium*, a death by stoning.

They barked and grunted and howled like ravenous

mongrels. With the fists of theirs hands they beat Him, bruising His face and rattling His teeth. With the roughest of violence, they dragged Him to a pillar, wrenching His shoulders, and tearing His muscles; as commanded by Pontius Pilate, they lashed him to the pillar, that served no other purpose on this earth, not to support a structure, instead to support the suffering of the condemned to scourging.

He clutched at the pillar like unto the rock in the garden of Gethsemene, pleading with God, praying without betraying neither a sound nor his despair, "O! My Father, Thou Hath given Me a cup, shall I not drink it?" With His back exposed that He should suffer for righteousness' sake, happy was He? but most afraid He was of His terror, He was troubled, and His body quivered and quaked.

Two Roman Mongrels took up the arms of rods of wood and stood one and the another on the sides of Him. He turned His face to find in the crowd, His Mother, Mary and He saith, "Cry not, Mother, for the Son of man must suffer many things, and be rejected of the elders and chief priests and scribes, and be crucified, and be raised the third day."

And Mary, His Mother and the Mother of God the Most High, dropped to her knees in the very spot where a river of her Son's blood would flow, and prayed a prayer of Prophecy, "Who hath believed our report? and to whom is the arm of the LORD revealed? For He shall grow up before Him as a tender plant, and as a root out of a dry ground: He hath no form nor comeliness; and when we shall see Him, there is no beauty that we should desire Him. He is despised and rejected of men—" Then His mother remembereth all they in the synagogue, when they heard these things, were filled with wrath, and rose up, and thrust Him out of the city, and led **Him** unto the brow of the hill whereon their city had been built, that they might cast him down headlong, but **He** passing through the midst of them went **His** way. Howbeit lashed to the pillar, **He** could not, nor would not pass through the midst of them.

And the Roman Alpha Mongrel, who leadeth, barked his counting, *"Unus!"* And a ferocious and rapacious Roman Mongrel, thirsty for blood and gluttonous for flesh, struck **Him** with a rod of wood and a stripe of injured flesh bruised on **His** body. The suddenness of the shock of the scourging, the sting of the pain, distressed **Him**. Prepared for this moment since the beginnings of **His** ministry **He** thought **He** was, but prepared **He** was not for the piercing pain for though being in the form of **God**, and being found in fashion as a man, **He** is humbling **Himself**, and being obedient unto death, even the death of the cross. But the agony only now came to pass and **He** must endure and be endured.

And continued Mary did her prayer, "A man of sorrows, and acquainted with grief–" **whereas** in the garden, **His** soul sorrowed exceeding, even unto death.

The Barker counteth, *"Duo!"* And the other Roman Mongrel struck with his own rod, striping **His** flesh fresh with bruises. **He** sought to pray to **His Father**, but his mind was asudden a fiery Inferno of pain.

Mary lamented, "And we hid as it were our faces from **Him**–" **whereas He** knoweth all **His** disciples forsook **Him**, and fled. And there followed **Him** a certain young man, having a linen cloth cast about his naked body; and the young men laid hold on him: and he left the linen cloth, and fled from them naked.

"Tres!" saith the Barker and a third stripe scourged, the welts of the first and the second blistered with water and

bled.

Mary cried, "He was despised, and we esteemed Him not—" *whereas* He could not silence the words remembered from of Simon Peter, the rock upon which He would build His Church: "I doth not know this Man of whom you speak. God shalt mend my soul if I lieth. God warrant me! I am not one with Him. A devil's name! bear not false witness against me. I am not nor ever hath been this Man's disciple!" He knew the knowledge that He hath been cursed at and sworn against and finally forsaken.

"*Quattuor!*" barked the Barker, and a groan escaped His lips as the Mongrel striped again, and the Roman Mongrels huffed through stained and jagged teeth, spital raining down upon Him.

Mary prayed, "Surely He hath borne our griefs—" *whereas* even when the even was come, they brought unto Him many that were possessed with devils.

And the Barker counteth, "*Quinque!*"

And Mary pleaded, "And carried our sorrows—" *whereas* by casting out the spirits with His word, and healed all that were sick.

"*Sex!*"

And Mary lamented, "Yet we did esteem Him stricken—" *whereas* the elders and the chief priests and the scribes hath answered and hath said, "He is guilty of death!"

"*Septem!*" And the third stripe and the fourth and the fifth blistered and the flesh split and blood issued forth. And He shrieked in the fiery Inferno of His mind, a silent prayer to His Father, "O! My Father, if it be possible, let this cup pass from Me! Please! I beseech Thee!"

Mary cried, "Smitten of God, and afflicted—" *whereas* the chief priests shalt mock Him, with the scribes and elders,

The Roman Mongrels scourge Him of His Flesh!

shalt say, "He saved others; Himself He cannot save. If He be the King of Israel, let Him now come down from the cross, and we will believe Him. He trusted in God; let Him deliver Him now, if He will have Him: for He said, 'I AM the Son of God.' "

"*Octo!*" And He wept. And He yelped.

Mary again cried, "But He was wounded for our transgressions–" *whereas* He hath made Him to be sin for us, who knew no sin; that we might be made the righteousness of God in Him.

"*Novem!*" saith the Barker, and a few of the Chaff saith, "We deny Him O! LORD. Crucify Him. We standeth not by Him. Crucify Him!"

Mary wept, "He was bruised for our iniquities–" *whereas* He, who was made a little lower than the angels for the suffering of death, crowned with glory and honour; that He by the grace of God should taste death for every man.

And the Roman Mongrels layeth aside their rods of white wood and took into their hands whips made of cords. The Barker howled, "*Decem!*"

Mary cast her eyes to the paved stones and prayed, "The chastisement of our peace was upon Him–" *whereas* He shalt maketh peace through the blood of His cross, by Him to reconcile all things unto Himself; by Him, I say, whether they be things in earth, or things in heaven.

"*Undecim!*" The knots of cords beat and bruised His flesh. Where knots of the nets of the fish they caught in the Sea of Galilee to be delivered onto the supper table, these knots caught His anguish and His agony to deliver Him onto the cross.

Mary cried, "And with His stripes we are healed–" *whereas* He shalt His own self bare our sins in His own body on the tree, that man, being dead to sins, should live unto righteousness: by whose stripes shalt be healed.

"*Duodecim!*" Many of the elders and the chief priests and the scribes abandoned their witnessing, in their weakness wounded were their souls for their transgressions against **Him**.

Mary again cried, "All we like sheep have gone astray–" ***whereas***, **He** is the propitiation for our sins: and not for ours only, but also for the sins of the whole world.

The Barker saith, "*Tredecim!*" and the whip bit into a blistered stripe and blood and water burst forth.

And Mary prayed, "We have turned every one to **His** own way; and the **LORD** hath laid on **Him** the iniquity of us all–" ***whereas*** **He** gave **Himself** for our sins, that **He** might deliver us from this present evil world, according to the will of **God** and our **Father**: Herein is love, not that we loved **God**, but that **He** loved us, and sent **His** Son to be the propitiation for our sins.

"*Quattuordecim!*" and when the whips made of cords striped the flesh of **His** back, **He** groaned and moaned again and the women whom were counted amongst **His** disciples wept, their empathy striping their own backs as their tears striped their faces with rivers of weeping.

Mary lamented, "**He** was oppressed, and **He** was afflicted–" ***whereas*** the Roman Mongrels shalt plat a crown of thorns, they shalt put it upon **His** head, with a reed in **His** right hand: and they shalt bow the knee before **Him**, and mock **Him**, saying, "Hail, **King of the Jews**!" And then shalt they spit upon **Him**, and take the reed, and smote **Him** on the head.

And the Barker counteth, "*Qindecim!*" and when the whips made of cords striped the flesh of **His** back, **He** again moaned and to the elders and the chief priests and the scribes, the moan to them sounded akin to a faithful cry of prayer.

Mary marvelled, "Yet he opened not **His** mouth—" *whereas* the Centurians hath heard Pilate say unto **Him**, "Hearest thou not how many things they witness against **Thee**?" And **He** answered him to never a word.

"*Sedicm!*" and **His** groaning took unto the air of supplication. How could it be the moans were not of anguish but of adoration?

Mary mourned, "**He** is brought as a **Lamb** to the slaughter—"

"*Septendecim!*" barked the Barker over the cries and bleating of the Paschal lambs being slaughtered rained upon Jerusalem! For the life of the flesh is in the blood: and **He** have given it to you upon the altar to make an atonement for your souls: for it is the blood that maketh an atonement for the soul.

And Mary prayed, "And as a sheep before her shearers is dumb—" *whereas* ye know that ye were not redeemed with corruptible things, as silver and gold, from our vain conversation received by tradition from our fathers; but with the precious blood of **Christ**, as of a **Lamb** without blemish and without spot:

"*Dueodevignti!*" but the Paschal lambs knew their days of service were ended for in **His** Son manifested the love of **God** toward us, because that **God** sent **His** only begotten Son into the world, that we might live through **Him**. Herein is love, not that we loved **God**, but that **He** loved us, and sent **His** Son to be the propitiation for our sins. Beloved, if **God** so loved us, we ought also to love one another.

And Mary again marvelled, "So he openeth not **His** mouth—" *whereas* the Chaff saw **He** answered Pilate to never a word; insomuch that the governor marvelled greatly.

"*Undevignti!*"

And Mary cried, "He was taken from prison and from judgment–" **whereas** the elders and the chief priests and the scribes knoweth of the prison of their flesh, but knoweth not they shalt all appear before the judgment seat of **Christ**; that every one may receive the things done in **His** body, according to that **He** hath done, whether it be good or bad.

The Barker barketh, *"Viginti!"* and the twentieth stripe buckled **His** knees and **He** clutched at the iron rings as the pain and agony overcame **Him**. And summoned **He His** strength.

The Roman Mongrels cast aside their whips made of cords and having cast aside their rods of white wood, instead maketh use of a different species of rod, a thorned rod, knotted and splintered.

And Mary pleaded, "And who shall declare **His** generation?–" **whereas** the generation who shall not pass, till all these things be fulfilled stood in their own horror and agony as living witnesses to the flaying of **His** flesh, and the shedding of **His** Blood, but they beholdeth not the Lamb of **God**, which taketh away the sin of the world!

"Unus et viginti!" barked the Barker and the Roman lashed **Him** with such natural implements of torture and tore at **His** flesh. And a cry of agony escaped **His** lips, *"Eloi!"* and in the fiery Inferno of **His** mind, **He** cried, *"Lama sabachthani?"*

"For **He** was cut off out of the land of the living "

"Duo et Viginti!" The second Dog scourged **Him** of **His** flesh, and blood poured from the wound, staining **His** arms scarlet

Mary again cried, "For the transgression of **His** people was **He** stricken–"

"Tres et Viginti!" and ribbons were flayed from **His**

flesh and an elder of the chief priests prayed silently to the LORD God of Israel to have mercy on Him.

"And He made His grave with the wicked, and with the rich in His death–" **whereas** a rich man, a Pharisee of Arimathaea named Joseph, who stood amongst not amongst the elders and chief priests and scribes, but with the women whom count as His disciples, knew his mission was to goeth to Pilate and beg for the Him body and taketh then the Body and wrap it in clean linen cloth, and lay it in his own new tomb, which he had hewn out in the rock: and rolleth a great stone to door the sepulchre, only then to depart. But he could not depart his Master, though the violence done to Him wounded His soul, though Joseph in fullest knowledge that He needeth only but once suffer for Joseph's sins, the just for the unjust, that He shalt bring us to God, being put to death in the flesh, but quickened by the Spirit: He is the propitiation for the Arimathaean's sins: and not for his only, but also for the sins of the whole world.

"*Quattuor et Viginti!*" And a cry of agony escaped His lips, "*Eloi!*" and again in the fiery Inferno of His mind, He screamed, "*Lama sabachthani?*" His knees shuddered His muscles trembled, His heart pounded and the strength goeth out of His calfs. He clutched at the iron rings and struggled to stand knowing His suffering the scourging for our sins would not abate.

"Because He had done no violence–" The elders and chief priests and scribes hath head Pontius Pilate saith unto them, "I find in Him no fault at all."

"*Quinque et Viginti!*" and the thorns of the thorned rod gnashed at His flesh as if were they teeth, gnawing and growling like a rabid hound.

"Neither was any deceit in His mouth–" He suffered the scouring because He is suffering for us, leaving us an example, that ye should follow **His** steps: **Who** did no sin, neither was guile found in **His** mouth: **Who**, when **He** is reviled, reviled not again; suffering now **He** threatens not; but commits **Himself** to **Him** that judgeth righteously: **Who His** own self shalt bare our sins in **His** own body on the tree, that we, being dead to sins, should live unto righteousness: by **Whose** stripes ye were healed.

"Sex et Viginti!" The scourging closed **His** eyes and opened **His** mouth to moan, to groan, to sigh, to cry and yet no sound could be heard by mortal ears, but the angels of the **LORD** heard **His** the lamenting, whom wept in their own lamentations.

"Yet it pleased the **LORD** to bruise **Him**–"
"Septem et Viginti!"
"**He** hath put **Him** to grief–"
"Duodetriginta!" The Roman Mongrel flogged **Him**, the knots of the thorned rod breaketh the bruises unto the skin of **His** flesh, flooding blood over the organs of **His** flesh.

"When **Thou** shalt make **His** soul an offering for sin–" **He** redeemed us from the curse of the law, being made a curse for us: for it is written, "**His** body shall not remain all night upon the tree, but thou shalt in any wise bury **Him** that day; (for he that is hanged is accursed of **God**;) that thy land be not defiled, which the **LORD** thy **God** giveth thee for an inheritance".

"Undetriginta!" howled the Barker, and the knotted and splintered rod tore at **His** flesh of **His** buttocks. And a cry of agony escaped the fiery Inferno of **His** mind and through **His** mouth, *"Lama sabachthani?"*

"He shall see **His** seed, he shall prolong **His** days–"
The Barker barketh, *"Triginta!"* and the Roman Mongrels scourged **Him** of **His** flesh again.

"And the pleasure of the LORD shall prosper in His hand–" ***whereas*** He hath lifted up His eyes to heaven, and said, "Father, the hour is come; glorify Thy Son, that Thy Son also may glorify Thee: as Thou hast given Him power over all flesh, that He should give eternal life to as many as Thou hast given Him. And this is life eternal, that they might know thee the only true God, and Jesus Christ, whom Thou hast sent. I have glorified Yhee on the earth: I have finished the work which Thou gavest Me to do. And now, O! Father, glorify Thou Me with Thine own self with the glory which I had with Thee before the world was."

"*Unus et Trignita!*"

"He shall see of the travail of His soul–" ***whereas*** He was in Bethsaida of the Galilee when there were certain Greeks among them that came up to worship at the feast came unto Philip, when He hath saith unto them , "The hour is come, that the Son of man should be glorified. Verily, verily, I say unto you, except a corn of wheat fall into the ground and die, it abideth alone: but if it die, it bringeth forth much fruit. He that loveth his life shall lose it; and he that hateth his life in this world shall keep it unto life eternal. If any man serve Me, let him follow Me; and where I am, there shall also My servant be: if any man serve Me, him will My Father honour. Now is My soul troubled; and what shall I say? Father, save Me from this hour: but for this cause came I unto this hour. Father, glorify Yhy name. Then came there a voice from heaven, saying, 'I have both glorified it, and will glorify it again.' "

"*Duo et Trignita!*" And when the Roman Mongrel scourged Him splinters of the thorned rod splintered into His flesh like unto nails of the crucifixion.

Mary prayed, "And shall be satisfied: by His knowledge shall my righteous servant justify many—" *whereas* **God** commendeth His love toward us, in that, while we were yet sinners, **Christ** died for us. Much more then, being now justified by His blood, we shall be saved from wrath through Him.

And the Roman Mongrels abandoned the broken and now thornless thorned rods, to seize in their mongrel fists straps of leather arrayed with metal balls and adorned with shards of bone and the Barker howled, *"Tres et Trignita"* and the metal balls embeddened into His flesh and the bones bit into His bones.

"For He shall bear their iniquities—" *whereas* He is offering to bear the sins of many; and unto them that look for Him shall he appear the second time without sin unto salvation.

"Quattuor et Trignita!" As His flesh tore and His blood ruptured by the Roman Mongrels' implements of torture, He tried in His tiredness to remember the Words of His Father, "Sorrow is better than laughter: for by the sadness of the countenance the heart is made better." But His love for the Father in this moment eclipsed the sun with the moon of the agony of this affliction.

"Therefore will He divide Him a portion with the great—"

"Quinque et Trignita!" His sufferance in the scouring, the agony of His affection was He afflictcd for all our affliction, and the angel of His presence He shalt save them: in His love and in His pity He is redeeming them; and He is baring them, and He is carrying them all the days of old.

"And He shall divide the spoil with the strong—" *whereas* on a mountain in the Galilee, He appointed them and spake unto them saying, "All power is given unto Me in heaven and in earth. Go ye therefore, and teach all nations, baptizing them in the name of the Father, and of the Son, and of the Holy Ghost: teaching them to observe all things whatsoever I have commanded you: and, lo, I am with you always, even unto the end of the world. Amen.”

"*Sex et Trignita!*" The whip of metal and bone wrenched His flesh and His bone, and writhing in His labour pains giving birth to a New Covenant with man, for rememberth His words: “A woman when she is in travail hath sorrow, because her hour is come: but as soon as she is delivered of the child, she remembereth no more the anguish, for joy that a man is born into the world. And ye now therefore have sorrow: but I will see you again, and your heart shall rejoice, and your joy no man taketh from you.”

"Because He hath poured out His soul unto death—" *whereas* when it shall be about the sixth hour of His crucifixion, there shall be a darkness over all the earth until the ninth hour. And the sun shalt be darkened, and the veil of the temple shalt be rent in the midst. And He shalt cry with a loud voice, He said, “Father, into thy hands I commend My spirit”: and having said thus, He shalt give up the ghost.

"*Septem et Trignita!*" He could suffer these stripes but what pained Him most in His agony is His knowing the knowledge that His disciples shalt endure afflictions, doing the work of an evangelist, making full proof of thy ministry; enduring hardness, as His good soldier of; they therefore are not ashamed of His testimony: but are the partakers of the afflictions of the gospel according to the power of God.

"And He was numbered with the transgressors—" *whereas* the scripture shalt fulfilled, when they with Him

---

The Roman Mongrels “worship” Him!

shalt crucify two thieves; the one on **His** right hand, and the other on **His** left.

"Deuodequadraginta!" But **His** heart rejoices in the hardship of **His** flesh's lacerations that it shall come to pass that when one member suffers, all the members suffers with it; or one member be honoured, all the members rejoice with it.

"And **He** bare the sin of many–" ***whereas* He His** own self shalt bare our sins in **His** own body on the tree, that we, being dead to sins, should live unto righteousness: by whose stripes ye were healed.

"Undequadraginta!" **He** willingly suffered the scourging of **His** flesh torn from **His** bones, the rending of **His** muscles, and the rupturing of **His** blood, and the agony coursing through **His** veins, because **His** disciples shalt glory in tribulations also: knowing that tribulation worketh patience; approving themselves as the ministers of **God**, in much patience, in afflictions, in necessities, in distresses, in stripes, in imprisonments, in tumults, in labours, in watchings, in fastings; by pureness, by knowledge, by long suffering, by kindness, by the **Holy Ghost**, by love unfeigned, by the word of truth, by the power of **God**, by the armour of righteousness on the right hand and on the left, by honour and dishonour, by evil report and good report: as deceivers, and yet true; as unknown, and yet well known; as dying, and, behold, we live; as chastened, and not killed; as sorrowful, yet alway rejoicing; as poor, yet making many rich; as having nothing, and yet possessing all things. And when they are troubled on every side, yet not distressed; they are perplexed, but not in despair; for they light affliction, which is but for a moment, worketh for them a far more exceeding and eternal weight of glory; and their hope of us is stedfast, knowing, that as we are partakers of the sufferings, so shall

we be also of the consolation.

"And made intercession for the transgressors—" **whereas** it is **Christ** who shalt die, yea rather, shalt rise again, who shalt be even at the right hand of **God**, who also making an intercession for us.

"*Quadraginta!*—" And the Roman Mongrel in the beginning of his next scourging—

—And Saul of Tarsus screamed in torment for his very soul, "Forty stripes ye gaveth. Doth not exceed: If ye shouldst exceed and beat **Him**, I plead! I and my brothers should seem lewd unto the **LORD**!"

And the Roman Mongrels obeyed and laid down their implements of torture and gathered unto **Him**, the whole pack of Roman Mongrels. And they put on **Him His** own white robe without seam, woven from the top throughout, the blood of **His** scourging stained the robe through from head to foot in every thread in brilliant scarlet. And they spit upon **Him**, and took the reed in **His** right hand, and smote **Him** on the head. And the Mongrels platted a crown of thorns, and put it on **His** head, which causeth four rivers of blood to form the Pishon, Gihon, Hiddekel, and Phrath to water of garden of our Salvation. And the Mongrels put on **Him** a purple robe, and said, "Hail, **King of the Jews**!" and they smote **Him** with their hands, **His** cheeks bruised, **His** teeth rattled, and **His** eyes swoln with a flood of blood. ✠

Chapter 7
"Whom Shalt I Release Unto Ye?
Jesus Bar-Abba or
Jesus, Son of Abba"

**HEN HE COMETH FORTH,** wearing the crown of thorns, and the purple bloodstained robe and Pilate saith unto the Chaff and the Wheat, "Behold, the man!" Then when Pontius Pilate saw he prevailed not against this particular and peculiar multitude, and was wont to release unto the people a prisoner, whom they would. And they had imprisoned a notable insurrectionary, called Jesus Bar-Abba, which is interpreted, "the son of the father."

Pilate saith, "My custom during this feast of thine, I am wont to release unto the people a prisoner whom ye would. I hath a prisoner herewith who leadeth insurrection, is a demagogue and a thief and a murderer. Whom wilt ye that I release unto you? Jesus Bar-Abba, a confessed murderer and seditionist in conspiracy the *Scarii*, or He which calleth Himself the Son of the Father, likewise called the Christ?" He knew that for envy they had delivered Him.

When Pontius Pilate sees Him scourged of His flesh, he saith, "Ecce homo!"

Then Pilate sat down on the judgment seat, and Lo! his wife sent unto him, saying, "Have thou nothing to do with that just **Man**: for I have suffered many things this day in a dream because of **Him**: Why do the heathen rage, and the people imagine a vain thing? The kings of the earth set themselves, and the rulers take counsel together, against the **LORD**, and against **His** anointed, saying, 'Let us break their bands asunder, and cast away their cords from us.' **He** that sitteth in the heavens shall laugh: the **LORD** shall have them in derision. Then shall **He** speak unto them in **His** wrath, and vex them in **His** sore displeasure. 'Yet have I set **My** king upon **My** holy hill of Zion.' **He** will declare the decree: the **LORD** hath said unto **Him**, 'Thou art **My Son**; this day have I begotten **Thee**. Ask of **Me**, and I shall give **Thee** the heathen for **Thine** inheritance, and the uttermost parts of the earth for **Thy** possession. **Thou** shalt break them with a rod of iron; **Thou** shalt dash them in pieces like a potter's vessel.'

"Be wise now therefore, O! my husband: be instructed, ye judges of the earth. Serve the **LORD** with fear, and rejoice with trembling. Kiss the **Son**, lest **He** be angry, and ye perish from the way, when **His** wrath is kindled but a little. Blessed are all they that put their trust in **Him**."

But the chief priests and elders persuaded the Chaff that they should ask Jesus Bar-Abba, and destroy **Jesus**. And an aged man, their adversary the devil, as a roaring lion, walketh about the Praetorium, seeking whom he may devour and as the author of confusion sown confusion into the Wheat believing that the man named Jesus Bar-Abba, whom Pilate offered freedom unto was their Rabbi, **Jesus**, the **Son** of the **Father**. Many of the Wheat never knew the knowledge of the appearance of the Nazarene from the Galilee for **His** ministry was in the far country about the sea of Galilee, and thus the aged man, the god of this world, blinded the minds of them even which believe, lest the light of the glorious gospel of the **Son** of the **Father**, who is the image of **God**, should shine unto them. The aged man alone sowest great confusion in the Wheat.

The governor answered and said unto them, "Whether of the twain will ye that I release unto you?" And the Chaff chanted, "Bar-Abba. Bar-Abba. Bar-Abba. Bar-Abba"; the Chaff wished for the release of the insurrectionary. And the aged man got an advantage over the Wheat: for they were ignorant of his devices and the Wheat chanted, "Bar-Abba. Bar-Abba. Bar-Abba. Bar-Abba"; the Wheat believeth that Pilate heard, "The **Son** of the **Father**. The **Son** of the **Father**. The **Son** of the **Father**. The **Son** of the **Father**."

The ignorance of the intricacies of Aramaic cost **Him His** life for Pilate heard both the Chaff and the Wheat call upon the release of Jesus Bar-Abba and saith, "What shall I do then with **Him** which is called the **Son** of the **Father**?"

Saul of Tarsus saith unto his governor, "**His** blasphemy, the Word justifies **Him**! **He** the Messiah is not. Defy **Him**. The **False Prophet**, standeth ye not by **Him**. Speaking our truths, we cannot belie **Him**! **He** the **Messiah** is not. Decry **Him**." The Chaff all call unto Pilate, "We deny **Him** O! **LORD**. Crucify **Him**. We standeth not by **Him**. Crucify **Him**! We decry **Him** O! **LORD**. Crucify **Him**!"

And Pilate saith, "Shall I crucify your **King**?" And Saul bellowed in his blasphemy, "We hath no king but Caesar!" And the Chaff worshipped in that moment not the **LORD God of Israel**, but the Caesar whom sitteth on his seat over the seven hills of Rome, chanting, "We hath no king but Caesar! We hath no king but Caesar! We hath no king but Caesar! We hath no king but Caesar!—"

And the governor said, "Why, what evil hath **He** done?" But Chaff cried out the more, saying, "Let **Him** be crucified because **He** maketh **Himself** One with **God**!"

But the chief priests and elders persuaded the most loyal of the Chaff that they should ask for Bar-Abba, and destroy **Him**. The governor answered and said unto them, "Whether of the twain will ye that I release unto you?" And they cried out all at once, saying, "Away with this **Man**, and release unto us Jesus Bar-Abba." Then Pilate acquiesced to the mob and set free the insurrectionary.

The **Holy Ghost** inspired a sermon in that moment in the heart of Simon Peter, whom stood off afar and his soul sang these words, though he knoweth not the knowledge of the source, nor the day when, nor to whom, he would saith these words:

"Ye men of Israel, why marvel ye at this? or why look ye so earnestly on us, as though by our own power or holiness we had made a lame man to walk? The **God** of Abraham, and of Isaac, and of Jacob, the **God** of our fathers, hath glorified **His Son Jesus**; whom ye delivered up, and denied **Him** in the presence of Pilate, when he was determined to let **Him** go. But ye denied the **Holy One** and the **Just**, and desired a murderer to be granted unto you; and killed the **Prince of life**, whom **God** hath raised from the dead, whereof we are witnesses." The **Holy Ghost** said this to Peter though he believed not yet in the Resurrection of the dead. "And **His** name through faith in **His** name hath made this man strong, whom ye see and know: yea, the faith which is by him hath given **Him** this perfect soundness in the presence of you all.

"And now, brethren, I wot that through ignorance ye did it, as did also your rulers. But those things, which **God** before had shewed by the mouth of all **His** prophets, that the **Son** of the **Father** should suffer, **He** hath so fulfilled. Repent ye therefore, and be converted, that your sins may be blotted out, when the times of refreshing shall come from the presence of the **LORD**. And **He** shall send **Him**, which before was preached unto you: whom the **Heaven** must receive until the times of restitution of all things, which **God** hath spoken by the mouth of all **His** holy prophets since the world began. For Moses truly said unto the fathers, 'A prophet shall the **LORD** your **God** raise up unto you of your brethren, like unto me; **Him** shall ye hear in all things whatsoever **He** shall say unto you. And it shall come to pass, that every soul, which will not hear that prophet, shall be destroyed from among the people.' Yea, and all the prophets from Samuel and those that follow after, as many as have spoken, have likewise foretold of these days. Ye are the children of the prophets, and of the covenant which **God** made with our fathers, saying unto Abraham, 'And in thy seed shall all the kindreds of the earth be blessed.' Unto you first **God**, having raised up **His Son Jesus**, sent **Him** to bless you, in turning away every one of you from thy iniquities."

And Pilate gave sentence that it should be as they required. And he released unto them him that for sedition and murder from the cells of the prison, whom they had desired; but he delivered **Him** to their will.

When Pilate saw that he could prevail nothing, but that rather the Chaff make a tempestuous trantrum like children, he took water, and washed his hands before the multitude, saying, "I am innocent of the **Blood** of this just **Man**: see ye to it."

Then through the grace of the **Holy Ghost**, the Chaff swallowed the curse upon their lips, which wouldst say, "**His** blood be on us, and on our children." Said curse, which the devil deceived the bitter Matthew into its institution, on the morrow would verily condemneth generations of their children as crucifiers of the **Christ**. Knowing the knowledge that the aged man, who is called the devil and Satan, who deceives the whole world, desired the Chaff to raise up with one voice and forever wear the curse of blood, **He** saith instead in a singular and thunderous voice: "**How much more shall My blood, who through the Holy Ghost offer Myself without spot to God, purge your conscience from dead works to serve the living God? But if ye walk in the light, as ye are in the light, ye shall have fellowship one with another, and My blood cleanseth ye from all sin!**"

Forthwith, **He** turneth the water in the basin into wine and saith, "**For this is My blood of the New Covenant, which is shed for many for the remission of sins. Take heed therefore unto yourselves, and to all the flock, over the which the Holy Ghost hath made you overseers, to feed the church of God, which I hath purchased with My own blood. In whom ye shall have redemption through My blood, the forgiveness of sins, according to the riches of My grace. And having made peace through the blood of My cross, by Me to reconcile all things unto myself; I say, whether they be things in earth, or things in heaven.**"

Prologue
"The Transfiguration"

ND IT HAD CAME TO PASS about an year before the elders and the chief priests and the scribes condemned **Him** to be crucified, **He** took Simon Peter and John and James, the sons of Zebedee, and went up into a mountain to pray. On the mountain stood a great oak of great strength that shouldst have been choked unto death by the vast brier of thorns which grew at its feet, that should be fulfilled of the Prophets saying: "Upon the land of my people shall come up thorns and briers; and the sin of Israel, shall be destroyed: the thorn and the thistle shall come up on their altars."

And as **He** prayed: **"Why do the heathen rage, and the people imagine a vain thing? The kings of the earth set themselves, and the rulers take counsel together, against the LORD, and against His anointed, saying,**

'Let us break their bands asunder, and cast away their cords from us.' He that sitteth in the heavens shall laugh: the LORD shall have them in derision. Then shall He speak unto them in His wrath, and vex them in His sore displeasure. Yet have I set My king upon My holy hill of Zion. I will declare the decree: the Lord hath said unto Me, 'Thou art my Son; this day have I begotten thee. Ask of me, and I shall give thee the heathen for thine inheritance, and the uttermost parts of the earth for thy possession. Thou shalt break them with a rod of iron; thou shalt dash them in pieces like a potter's vessel.' Be wise now therefore, O! ye kings: be instructed, ye judges of the earth. Serve the Lord with fear, and rejoice with trembling. Kiss the Son, lest He be angry, and ye perish from the way, when His wrath is kindled but a little. Blessed are all they that put their trust in Him."

And angels of the LORD appeared in the Heavens to disrobe Him of His earthly countenance from the heavenly, and when rebelled against the angels of the LORD did the Devils of the earth, whom appeared as severed forearms and disrobed His earthly countenance of the skin of His flesh. And the soldiers of Hell took His robe of His flesh, flayed with hell-forged blades without a single tear; and the limbs of the Devils therefore fighting amongst themselves nearly renting His robe of the skin of His flesh, beheretofore queerly casting lots: so that that the scripture *might* sacrilegiously be fulfilled, which saith, "They parted my raiment among them, and for my vesture they did cast lots." These things therefore the soldiers of Hell did.

The hands of the severed flayed forearms of the Devils lashed Him to the great, mighty oak with the thorns of the vast brier so that it would be fulfilled of the Prophets that **Christ** hath redeemed us from the curse of the law, being made a curse for us: for it is written, "**His** body shall not remain all night upon the tree, but thou shalt in any wise bury **Him** that day; (for he that is hanged is accursed of **God**;) that thy land be not defiled, which the **Lord** thy **God** giveth thee for an inheritance."

The Devils filleted **Him** of **His** flesh and took the meat and sacrileged it by cooking **His** flesh over a fissure of hell's fire in the earth, and gave **His** flesh amongst themselves, and said mockingly, "Take, eat; this is **His** body." And they laughed heartily. And they took a cup, and drained a vein of **His** blood and gave it amongst themselves, saying, "Drink ye all of it; for this is **His** blood of the new testament, which is shed for many for the remission of sins." The cackling of their laughter rose to a mighty din! Their unholy Communion mocketh **Him**!

And an angel of the **LORD** appeared unto **Him** in a flame of fire out of the midst of the bush of the brier of thorns: and the Devils looked, and, behold, the bush of the brier burned with fire, and the flames consumed not the bush, though fire and flame alighted the stout oak. The muscles of **His** flesh charred and seared. The smoke of salvation and stench of righteousness from the assault on not only **His** humanity but **His** divinity were a **Blessing** of the power and coming of **Him**, for **He** received from **God the Father** honour and glory. As the immolation of our **Lord** and **Saviour** reached a conflagration, the thorns released their grasp on **Him**, and the fashion of **His** countenance altered, and **His** raiment white and glistering. And behold! the Devils crawled back into the fissures of the earth and, behold! **He** prayed:

"**The Lord reigneth; let the people tremble: He**

sitteth between the cherubims; let the earth be moved. The Lord is great in Zion; and He is high above all the people. Let them praise Thy great and terrible name; for it is holy. The king's strength also loveth judgment; Thou dost establish equity, Thou executest judgment and righteousness in Jacob. Exalt ye the LORD our God, and worship at His footstool; for He is holy. Moses and Aaron among His priests, and Samuel among them that call upon His name; they called upon the LORD, and He answered them. He spake unto them in the cloudy pillar: they kept His testimonies, and the ordinance that He gave them. Thou answeredst them, O! Lord our God: Thou wast a God that forgavest them, though Thou tookest vengeance of their inventions. Exalt the LORD our God, and worship at His holy hill; for the Lord our God is holy!"

When therefore there talked with **Him** two men, which were Moses and Elias, which fulfilled of the Prophets, for it is written: "Behold, I will send you Elijah the prophet before the coming of the great and dreadful day of the LORD: and he shall turn the heart of the fathers to the children, and the heart of the children to their fathers, lest I come and smite the earth with a curse"; and when once the LORD had spake to Moses concerning the role of Aaron that he should shall take of the blood of the bullock, and sprinkle it with his finger upon the mercy seat eastward; and before the mercy seat shall he sprinkle of the blood with his finger seven times. Then shall he kill the goat of the sin offering, that is for the people, and bring his blood within the vail, and do with that blood as he did with the blood of the bullock, and sprinkle it upon the mercy seat, and before the mercy seat: And he shall make an atonement for the holy place, because of the uncleanness of the children of Israel, and because of their transgressions in all their sins: and so shall he do for the tabernacle of the congregation, that remaineth among them in the midst of their uncleanness.

"But!" Elijah prophesied, "But! **Christ** being come an high priest of good things to come, by a greater and more perfect tabernacle, not made with hands, that is to say, not of this building; neither by the blood of goats and calves, but by **His** own blood **He** entered in once into the holy place, having obtained eternal redemption for us. For if the blood of bulls and of goats, and the ashes of an heifer sprinkling the unclean, sanctifieth to the purifying of the flesh: How much more shall the blood of **Christ**, who through the eternal **Spirit** offered himself without spot to **God**, purge your conscience from dead works to serve the living **God**? And for this cause **He** is the **Mediator** of the new testament, that by means of death, for the redemption of the transgressions that were under the first testament, they which are called might receive the promise of eternal inheritance."

"For where a testament is," Moses proclaimed of the Law of the New Covenant, "there must also of necessity be the death of the testator. For a testament is of force after men are dead: otherwise it is of no strength at all while the testator liveth. Whereupon neither the first testament was dedicated without blood. For when I, Moses, had spoken every precept to all the people according to the law, he took the blood of calves and of goats, with water, and scarlet wool, and hyssop, and sprinkled both the book, and all the people, saying, 'This is the blood of the testament which **God** hath enjoined unto you.' Moreover he sprinkled with blood both the tabernacle, and all the vessels of the ministry. And almost all things are by the law purged with blood;

and without shedding of blood is no remission."

But Peter and they that were with Him were heavy with sleep: and when they suddenly awoken, they saw His glory, and the two men that stood with Him.

And it came to pass, as they departed from him, Peter said unto Him, "Master, it is good for us to be here: and let us make three tabernacles; one for Thee, and one for Moses, and one for Elias": not knowing what he said.

While he thus spake, there came a bright cloud, and overshadowed them: and they feared as they entered into the cloud. And there came a voice out of the cloud, saying, "This is my beloved Son: hear ye Him." And when the disciples heard it, they fell on their face, and were sore afraid. And when the voice was past, He was found alone. And He came and touched them, and said, "Arise, and be not afraid." And when they had lifted up their eyes, they saw no man, save Him only. And they kept it close, and as they came down from the mountain, He charged them, saying, "Tell the vision to no man, until the Son of man be risen again from the dead."

And His disciples asked Him, saying, "Why then say the scribes that Elijah must first come?" And He answered and said unto them, "Elijah truly shall first come, and restore all things. But I say unto you, that Elijah is come already, and they knew him not, but have done unto him whatsoever they listed. Likewise shall also the Son of man suffer of them." Then the disciples understood that He spake unto them of the Baptizer.

Chapter 8
"Via the Way of Grief"

THE WOMEN, WHO ACCOMPAny Mary, the Mother of God, Mary the Magdalene, and John, the disciple whom He loved, as they shadow Him on the way of His grief, prayed, "O! most merciful Jesus, with a contrite heart and penitent spirit, I bow down in profound humility before Thy divine majesty. I adore Thee as my supreme Lord and Master; I believe in Thee, I hope in Thee, I love Thee above all things. I am heartily sorry for having offended Thee, my Supreme and Only Good. I resolve to amend my life, and although I am unworthy to obtain mercy, yet the sight of Thy holy cross, on which Thou didst die, inspires me with hope and consolation. I will, therefore, meditate on Thy sufferings, and visit the stations of Thy Passion in company with Thy sorrowful Mother and my guardian an-

120

St. Francis of Assissi *The Way of the Cross*, abridged, adapted from, and expanded

gel, with the intention of promoting **Thy** honor and saving my soul.

"I desire to gain all the indulgences granted for this holy exercise for myself and for the Poor Souls in Purgatory. O! merciful **Redeemer**, who has said, *'And I, if I be lifted from earth, will draw all things to Myself,'* draw my heart and my love to **Thee**, that I may perform this devotion as perfectly as possible, and that I may live and die in union with **Thee**. Amen.

"We adore **Thee**, O! **Christ**, and we praise **Thee**, because by **Thy** holy cross, **Thou** hast redeemed the world."

And Mary the Magdalene prayed, "**Jesus**, most innocent, who neither did nor could commit a sin, was condemned to death, and moreover, to the most ignominious death of the cross. To remain a friend of Caesar, Pilate delivered **Him** into the hands of **His** enemies. A fearful crime — to condemn **Innocence** to death, and to offend **God** in order not to displease men!"

"O! innocent **Jesus**," the women prayed, "having sinned, I am guilty of eternal death, but **Thou** willingly dost accept the unjust sentence of death, that I might live. For whom, then, shall I henceforth live, if not for **Thee**, my **Lord**? Should I desire to please men, I could not be **Thy** servant. Let me, therefore, rather displease men and all the world, than not please **Thee**, O! **Jesus**.

And the Magdalene prayed, "When our divine **Saviour** beheld the cross, **He** most willingly stretched out **His** bleeding arms, lovingly embraced it, and tenderly kissed it, and placing it on **His** bruised shoulders, **He**, although almost exhausted, joyfully carried it."

"O! my **Jesus**, I cannot be **Thy** friend and follower, if I refuse to carry the cross. O! dearly beloved cross! I embrace thee, I kiss thee, I joyfully accept thee from the hands of my

God. Far be it from me to glory in anything, save in the cross of my **Lord** and **Redeemer**. By it the world shall be crucified to me and I to the world, that I may be **Thine** forever," prayed the women.

"Our dear **Saviour**," the Magdalene observed, "carrying the cross, was so weakened by its heavy weight as to fall exhausted to the ground. Our sins and misdeeds were the heavy burden which oppressed **Him**: the cross was to **Him** light and sweet, but our sins were galling and insupportable."

And the women prayed, "O! my **Jesus**, **Thou** didst bear my burden and the heavy weight of my sins. Should I, then, not bear in union with **Thee**, my easy burden of suffering and accept the sweet yoke of **Thy** commandments? **Thy** yoke is sweet and **Thy** burden is light: I therefore willingly accept it. I will take up my cross and follow **Thee**."

And the Magdalene lamented, "How painful and how sad it must have been for Mary, the sorrowful Mother, to behold her beloved **Son**, laden with the burden of the cross! What unspeakable pangs her most tender heart experienced! How earnestly did she desire to die in place of **Jesus**, or at least with **Him**! Implore this sorrowful Mother that she assist you in the hour of your death."

And the women prayed, "O! **Jesus**, O! Mary, I am the cause of the great and manifold pains which pierce your loving hearts! Oh, that also my heart would feel and experience at least some of your sufferings! O! Mother of Sorrows, let me participate in the sufferings which thou and **Thy Son** endured for me, and let me experience thy sorrow, that afflicted with thee, I may enjoy thy assistance in the hour of my death."

The Roman Mongrels compelled Simon of Cyrene to

Jesus faills and Simon of Cyrene is compelled!

help **Him** carry **His** cross, and **He** accepted his assistance. How willingly would **He** also permit you to carry the cross: **He** calls, but you hear **Him** not; **He** invites you, but you decline. What a reproach, to bear the cross reluctantly!

And the women again prayed, "O! **Jesus**! Whosoever does not take up **His** cross and follow **Thee**, is not worthy of **Thee**. Behold, I join **Thee** in the Way of **Thy** Cross; I will be **Thy** assistant, following **Thy** bloody footsteps, that I may come to **Thee** in eternal life. — **Lord Jesus**, crucified, have mercy on us!"

Veronica, impelled by devotion and compassion, presents her veil to **Him** to wipe **His** disfigured face. And **He** imprints on it **His** holy countenance: a great recompense for so small a service. What return to you make to your **Saviour** for **His** great and manifold benefits?

And the women continueth their prayer, "Most merciful **Jesus**! What return shall I make for all the benefits **Thou** hast bestowed upon me? Behold I consecrate myself entirely to **Thy** service. I offer and consecrate to **Thee** my heart: imprint on it **Thy** sacred image, never again to be effaced by sin."

He suffering, under the weight of **His** cross, again falls to the ground; but the cruel executioners do not permit **Him** to rest a moment. Pushing and striking **Him**, they urge **Him** onward. It is the frequent repetition of our sins which oppress **Him**. Witnessing this, how can I continue to sin?

And the women prayed unendingly, "O! **Jesus**, **Son** of David, have mercy on me! Offer me **Thy** helping hand, and aid me, that I may not fall again into my former sins. From this very moment, I will earnestly strive to reform: never-

Veronica and her blood-stained veil!

more will I sin! **Thou**, O! sole support of the weak, by **Thy** grace, without which I can do nothing, strengthen me to carry out faithfully this my resolution."

These devoted women, moved by compassion, weep over the suffering **Saviour**. But **He** turns to them, saying: **"Weep not for Me, Who am innocent, but weep for yourselves and for your children. For, behold, the days are coming, in the which they shall say, 'Blessed are the barren, and the wombs that never bare, and the paps which never gave suck.' Then shall they begin to say to the mountains, ' on us; and to the hills, 'Cover us.' For if they do these things in a green tree, what shall be done in the dry?"** Weep thou also, for there is nothing more pleasing to our **Lord** and nothing more profitable for thyself, than tears shed from contrition for thy sins.

"O! **Jesus**," the women called upon, "Who shall give to my eyes a torrent of tears, that day and night I may weep for my sins? I beseech **Thee**, through **Thy** bitter and bloody tears, to move my heart by **Thy** divine grace, so that from my eyes tears may flow abundantly, and that I may weep all my days over **Thy** sufferings, and still more over their cause, my sins.

Arriving exhausted at the foot of Calvary, **He** falls for the third time to the ground. **His** love for us, however, is not diminished, not extinguished. What a fearfully oppressive burden our sins must be to cause **Him** to fall so often! Had **He**, however, not taken them upon **Himself**, they would have plunged us into the abyss of Hell.

"Most merciful **Jesus**," the women beseeched, "I return **Thee** infinite tanks for not permitting me to continue in sin and to fall, as I have so often deserved, into the depths of Hell. Enkindle in me an earnest desire of amendment; let

His *flayed flesh is nailed to the cross!*

me never again relapse, but vouchsafe me the grace to persevere in penance to the end of my life.

When Our **Saviour** came unto a place called Golgotha, that is to say, "The place of the skull," the Mongrels cruelly despoiled **Him** of **His** garments. How painful this must have been because they adhered to **His** wounded and torn body, and with them parts of **His** bloody and tattered flesh were removed! All of **His** wounds were renewed. Hence they had despoiled **Him** of **His** garments, **He** might die possessed of nothing; how happy will **He** also die after laying aside **His** former self with all evil desires and sinful inclinations! And **His** nakedness was exposed so that Isaiah might be fulfilled, "**Thy** nakedness shall be uncovered, yea, **Thy** shame shall be seen: **I** will take vengeance, and **I** will spare not nor pity no man." And a like wise the elders and the chief priests and the scribes were themselves shamed by **His** nakedness, but they dared not speak lest they suffer the wrath and retribution of the Romans.

"Induce me, O! **Jesus**, to lay aside my former self and to be renewed according to **Thy** will and desire. I will not spare myself, however painful this should be for me: despoiled of things temporal, of my own will, I desire to die, in order to live for **Thee** forever," the women urged.

The Mongrels violently threw **Him**, being stripped of **His** garments, upon the cross. The splinters of the rough hewn wood pierced the stripes upon his back, lacerating **His** flesh and resumed the eager flood of blood. The Roman Mongrel with a ludicrous smile seized an iron nine-inch nail and hammered the spike into **His** wrist and a flash of lightning streaked through **His** body as lightning likewise flashed through the cloudless sky. The thunderbolts tightened the muscles of **His** hands, **His** arms, **His** chest, the veins of **His** blood throbbed as **His** Blood seeped down the spike, through the stout wood, and into the dust of the earth. With each of the hammer's strike, He shuddered and He spasmed, until the Roman Mongrel knew the fullness of his torturous knowledge His wrist was secured and immovable and moved then on to His other wrist and His suffering sustained is each subsequent strike of the spoke through his left wrist. Then His feet were nailed thereto to a wooden block, a parody of support whose very design was but to prolong the suffering of the crucified and to defuse any further sedition in His disciples.

In such excruciating pains He remained relentlessly silent, because it pleased His heavenly Father. He suffered patiently, because He suffered for Me. How do I act in sufferings and in troubles? How fretful and impatient, how full of complaints I AM!

"Father!" He prayed and lamented, "forgive them: for they know not what they do."

And the women lamented, "O! Jesus, gracious Lamb of God, I renounce forever my impatience. Crucify, O! Lord, my flesh and its concupiscences; scourge, scathe, and punish me in this world, do but spare me in the next. I commit my destiny to Thee, resigning myself to Thy holy will: may it be done in all things!"

And it was the third hour, and Behold! Jesus crucified! Behold His wounds, received for love of you! His whole appearance betokens love: His head is bent to kiss you; His arms are extended to embrace you; His Heart is open to receive you. O! superabundance of love, Jesus, the Son of God, dies upon the cross, that man may live and be delivered from everlasting death!

"O! most amiable Jesus!" the women beseeched, "Who will grant me that I may die for Thee! I will at least endeavor to die to the world. How must I regard the world and its vanities, when I behold **Thee** hanging on the cross, covered with wounds? O! **Jesus**, receive me into **Thy** wounded Heart: I belong entirely to **Thee**; for **Thee** alone do I desire to live and to die."

The Roman Mongrels gave **Him** sour wine mingled with gall to drink, in fulfilment of the Scripture where they shall give **Him** gall for **His** meat and in **His** thirst they give **Him** vinegar to drink, but when **He** had tasted it, **He** would not drink. But when **He** had tasted it. **He** would not drink.

They divided **His** garments, casting lots, that it might be fulfilled which was spoken by the prophet: "They part **My** garments among them, and cast lots upon **My** vesture." Sitting down, they kept watch over **Him** there. And thy put up over **His** head the accusation written against **Him** by Pilate: **JESUS OF NAZARETH THE KING OF THE JEWS**.

This title then read many of the Jews: for the place where **He** was crucified was nigh to the city: and it was written in Hebrew, and Greek, and Latin. Then said the elders, the chief priests and the scribes of the Jews said to Pilate, "Write not, 'THE KING OF THE JEWS'; but that **He** said, '**I AM KING OF THE JEWS.**' Pilate answered, "What I have written I have written."

And there were also two other, malefactors, led with **Him** to be put to death. And when they were come to the place, which is called Calvary. Then were there two thieves crucified with **Him**, one on the right hand, and another on the left. And saith one of the thieves, "If **Thou** be the **Christ**, save **Thyself** and us." And the other thief saith, "Dost not thou fear **God**? Speak! and ye confess! We hath committeth sins justly indeed;We receiveth due reward of our deeds. But this **Man** hath done not-a-thing amiss." And **He** then saith to the second, **"To day shalt thou with Me in paradise."**

And the elders and the chief priests and the scribes reviled **Him**, wagging their heads, and Saul of Tarsus, the Pharisee son of a Pharisee, and persecutor of **He**, saith, **"Thou**! **Thou** that destroyest the temple and buildest it in three days, save **Thyself**! If thou be the **Son of God**, come down from the cross. **He** saved others; **Himself He** cannot save. If **He** be the King of Israel, let **Him** now descend from the cross and we will see and believe **Him**. **He** trusted **God**; let **Him** deliver **Him** now, if **He** will have him: for **He** said, **'I AM the Son of God!'** "

Now there stood by the **His** cross **Him** mother, and **Him** mother's sister, Mary the wife of Cleophas, and Mary the Magdalene. When **He** therefore saw **His** mother, and the disciple standing by, whom **He** loved, **He** saith unto **His** mother, **"Woman, behold thy son!"** Then saith **He** to the disciple, **"Behold thy mother!"** And from that hour that disciple took her unto his own home.

And when the sixth hour was come, there was darkness over the whole land until the ninth hour. And at the ninth hour **Jesus** cried with a loud voice, saying, **"*Eloi, Eloi, lama sabachthani?*"** which is, being interpreted, **"**My **God**, my **God**, why hast thou forsaken me?**"**

And some of them that stood by, when they heard it, said, "Behold, he calleth Elias."

After this, knowing that all things were now accomplished, that the scripture might be fulfilled, **He** saith, **"I thirst."**

And Saul of Tarsus ran and filled from a vessel full of vinegar: and he filled a spunge with vinegar, and put it upon hyssop, and put it to **His** mouth to drink, saying, "Let alone; let us see whether Elias will come to take **Him** down."

He did not descend from the cross but remained on it until **He** died. And when taken down from it, **He** in death as in life, rested on the bosom of **His** divine Mother. Persevere in your resolutions of reform and do not part from the cross; he who persevereth to the end shall be saved. Consider, moreover, how pure the heart should be that receives the body and blood of **Christ** in the Adorable Sacrament of the Altar.

"It is finished!" He cried in a loud voice.

"O! **Lord Jesus**," the women whom were counted amongst **His** disciples cried, "**Thy** lifeless body, mangled and lacerated, found a worthy resting-place on the bosom of **Thy** virgin Mother. Have I not often compelled **Thee** to dwell in my heart, full of sin and impurity as it was? Create in me a new heart, that I may worthily receive **Thy** most sacred body in Holy Communion, and that **Thou** mayest remain in me and I in **Thee** for all eternity."

And **He** cried with a thunderous voice, **"Father, into thy hands I commend My spirit!"** and only then did **He** give up the ghost.

And when the centurion, which stood over against **Him**, saw that **He** so cried out, and gave up the ghost, the Roman Mongrel said, "Truly this man was the **Son of God**." ✞

The earth quaked at **Jesus**' *death, and the graves were opened and the corpses of the saints who had fallen asleep were raised and the dead walked!*

Chapter 9
"The Risen Dead"

WHEN HE CRIED WITH A LOUD voice, **"Father, into thy hands I commend My spirit!"** and gave up the ghost! The Jews, both of the chaff and of the wheat, therefore, because it was the preparation, that the bodies should not remain upon the cross on the sabbath day, (for that sabbath day was an high day,) besought Pilate that their legs might be broken, and that they might be taken away. Then came the soldiers, and they brake the legs of the first with a crack that resounded through the place of the skull like thunder, and the thief whom was crucified with **Him** cried out in the extremity of pain no longer able to stand upon the cross; his arms stretched and strained under his weight, ripping the flesh of his muscles and the bones of his wrists parted like the waters of the Red Sea at the nail that held him to the cross and his lungs lengthened and strained and cried out for breath, yet none would be given unto him and he gave of the ghost. And the soldiers went to the other thief crucified with **Him**, whom would see **He** that day in paradise and broke his legs, but the **LORD** sought pity upon him and he died without pain. But when they came to **Him**, and saw that **He** was dead already, they brake not **His** legs: but one of the soldiers with a spear pierced **His** side, and forthwith came there out blood and water. And he that saw it bare record, and his record is true: and he knoweth that he saith true, that ye might believe. For these things were done, that the scripture should be fulfilled, "A bone of **Him** shall not be broken". And again another scripture saith, "They shall look on **Him** whom they pierced."

And after this Joseph of Arimathaea, being a disciple of **His**, but secretly for fear of the Jews, besought Pilate that he might take away **His** body: and Pilate gave him leave. He came therefore, and took **His** body down from the cross.

And then the hosts of Heaven cried in their lamentations, their dark gloom penetrated the clouds, their cries the thunder, their weeping a torrent of rain, their fury and anger the lightning that struck the cross upon from which **He** had been taken down! And **God** cried out in a screaming and wailing heard by the entirety of the land of Israel as a crack of thunder so loud and so violent that the **LORD God of Israel** seized the moon in **His** raging and by the moon was the sun darkened as black as sackcloth of hair and the stars of **Heaven** and the constellations thereof gave not their light falling from **Heaven** in streaks and flashes, and the powers of the **Heavens** art shaken: and the moon caused not her light to shine, instead bleeding with blood.

And lightning bolted from the **Heavens** and struck

Joseph of Arimathea, a secret disciple of Jesus seeks His body from Pilate!

the True Cross, splintering it into a hail of nail-like splinters that rained down upon the elders and the chief priests and the scribes and the Roman Mongrels impaling and nailing them in their flesh. Thunderbolts of pain flashed through the bodies of the elders and the chief priests and the scribes as they winced and cried out to their LORD whilst a flood of their blood flowed out of their mortal wounds. The wounds of the Roman Mongrels whom crucified our **Lord and Saviour Jesus Christ** were as the poetic punishments and apt agonies of the Inferno for having murdered the **Son of God**.

And the LORD will punish the world for their evil, and the wicked for their iniquity; and the LORD will cause the arrogancy of the proud to cease, and will lay low the haughtiness of the terrible. And the LORD hath make a man, a **Son of Man**, more precious than fine gold; even a man than the golden wedge of Ophir. Therefore the LORD shook the heavens, and the earth shall remove out of her place, in the wrath of the LORD of hosts, and in the day of His fierce anger. And it shall be as the chased roe, and as a sheep that no man taketh up: they shall every man turn to His own people, and flee every one into His own land. Every one that is found shall be thrust through; and every one that is joined unto them shall fall by the sword. Their children also shall be dashed to pieces before their eyes; their houses shall be spoiled, and their wives ravished.

The angel of the LORD being glad in the whole armour of God, that he may be able to withstand in the evil day, and having done all, to stand. Stand therefore, having his loins girt about with truth, and having on the breastplate of righteousness; and his feet shod with the preparation of the gospel of peace; above all, taking the shield of faith, wherewith ye shall be able to quench all the fiery darts of the wicked. He descended from the heights of **Heaven** and with his fiery sword rent in twain from top to the bottom the veil of the temple:

And discovered he within the Holy of Holies an ungodly unholiness: where once there was a tabernacle made; the first, wherein once was the candlestick, and the table, and the shewbread; which is called the sanctuary. And after the second veil, the tabernacle which is called the Holy of Holies; which once had the golden censer, and the ark of the covenant overlaid round about with gold, wherein was the golden pot that had manna, and Aaron's rod that budded, and the tables of the covenant; and over it the cherubims of glory shadowing the mercyseat; of which we cannot now speak particularly.

And now! the Angel of the **LORD** discovered within the Holy of Holies the high-priest of the Sanhedrin, the Profaner of the **LORD** in a forbidden trial, profaned the sanctuary of **God** in unspeakable carnal acts with a harlot in the manner of a mongrel, her breasts heaving and swaying like the engorged udders of the sows in their sty. The high-priest turned but only his face to the angel of the **LORD** with hands bend in supplication, his sinful serpent still buried within the wicked wound of the woman, and he prayed in his trepidation and stark raving terror:

"Have mercy upon me, O! **God**, according to **Thy** lovingkindness: according unto the multitude of **Thy** tender mercies blot out my transgressions. Wash me throughly from mine iniquity, and cleanse me from my sin. For I acknowledge my transgressions: and my sin is ever before me.

Against Thee, Thee only, have I sinned, and done this evil in thy sight: that Thou mightest be justified when Thou speakest, and be clear when Thou judgest. Behold, I was shapen in iniquity; and in sin did my mother conceive me. Behold, Thou desirest truth in the inward parts: and in the hidden part Thou shalt make me to know wisdom. Purge me with hyssop, and I shall be clean: wash me, and I shall be whiter than snow. Make me to hear joy and gladness; that the bones which Thou hast broken may rejoice. Hide Thy face from my sins, and blot out all mine iniquities. Create in me a clean heart, O! God; and renew a right spirit within me. Cast me not away from thy presence; and take not thy Holy Ghost from me. Restore unto me the joy of Thy salvation; and uphold me with Thy free spirit. Then will I teach transgressors Thy ways; and sinners shall be converted unto Thee. Deliver me from bloodguiltiness, O! God, thou God of my salvation: and my tongue shall sing aloud of Thy righteousness. O! LORD, open Thou my lips; and my mouth shall shew forth Thy praise. For Thou desirest not sacrifice; else would I give it: Thou delightest not in burnt offering. The sacrifices of God are a broken spirit: a broken and a contrite heart, O! God, Thou wilt not despise. Do good in Thy good pleasure unto Zion: build Thou the walls of Jerusalem. Then shalt Thou be pleased with the sacrifices of righteousness, with burnt offering and whole burnt offering: then shall they offer bullocks upon Thine altar!"

     The adulterer against his LORD, who dared to spit a venomous Psalm from his sacrilegious mouth, instead bellowed in fear as the angel of the LORD held aloft his sword of Heaven, and rent the high-priest's most newest of vestments in twain to the very bone. Verily into the viscera. The cage of bones holding his heart opened like unto the gnashing maw of a great dragon, that old serpent, called the Devil, and Satan, which deceiveth the whole world; its fangs of rent ribs, dripping with blood, snarled in reserved roaring and snapped at the Angel of the LORD, whom denied to be fallen from Heaven, to be cut down to the ground, to weaken the nations accompanying Lucifer, the son of the morning! And the high-priest's bowels gushed out as most awful offal, and his bowels were loosed and maketh a sewer of the Sanctuary. The stench of his inequity made for most rancid incense.

The adulteress, the harlot, who defiled the Holy of Holies with her sex, cursed to be forever sick of her flowers, by the angel of the LORD, unclean until the great tribulation when shall the sun be darkened, and the moon shall not give her light, and the stars shall fall from heaven, and the powers of the Heavens shall be shaken: and then shall appear the sign of the Son of man in Heaven: and then shall all the tribes of the earth mourn, and they shall see the Son of man coming in the clouds of Heaven with power and great glory.

She wept in her wailing for she knew the curse of the LORD: that she lieth upon forever shall be unclean: every thing also that she sitteth upon shall be unclean. And whosoever toucheth her bed shall wash his clothes, and bathe himself in water, and be unclean until the last hour. And whosoever toucheth any thing that she sat upon shall wash his clothes, and bathe himself in water, and be unclean until the tribulation cometh. And if it be on her bed, or on any thing whereon she sitteth, when he toucheth it, he shall be unclean until last hour. And if any man lie with her at all, and her flowers be upon him, he shall be unclean until last hour; and all the bed whereon he lieth shall be unclean until last hour. Every bed whereon she lieth all the days of her issue shall be unto her as the bed of her separation: and whatsoever she sitteth upon shall be unclean, as the uncleanness until last hour. And whosoever toucheth those things shall be unclean, and shall wash his clothes, and bathe himself in water, and be unclean until the great tribulation cometh even.

As she wept and as she wailed, the issue of the harlot erupted from the scar of eve, a gash not unlike the wound of an axe, and deluged in an unending wave of issue and of an unnatural measure that burst through the door of the outer courtyard of Herod's Temple and cascaded down the steps, flooding the porch of the altar of burnt offerings. The priests and the sellers of the sacrifices, those who dared upright their tables of changing moneys and the seats from which they sold doves and sheep, drowned in the flood of blood, taking their last breathes in, not the Pool of Bethesda, the voluminous pool of the most vital of liquids; the cries of the sellers, the bleating of their sheep, all perishing in the crimson deep.

She besought the angel of the LORD to maketh an offer of a sin offering and the other for a burnt offering, and the angel of the LORD had mercy on the harlot, and sought to make an atonement for her before the LORD in defiance of the LORD's anger and the LORD's fury.

Therefore the angel of the LORD carried the body, rent in twain, of the high-priest through the diminishing flood of blood. The angel of the LORD offered the high-priest, a ravening wolf with blasphemous blemish, to be a burnt offering unto the LORD. And the priests of yore, Aaron's sons, now servants to the angels of the LORD, who descended from Heaven on the wings of crows upon their backs, taketh the blood of the high-priest, and put it upon the horns of the altar with their finger, and poured all the

blood beside the bottom of the altar. And the sons of Aaron flayed the flesh of the high-priest, and his skin, and his seed of Moloch, and they burned with fire without the temple: it is a sin offering. And the sons of Aaron put fire upon the altar, and lay the wood in order upon the fire: and then the sons of Aaron cut the high-priest in pieces, and wash the inwards of him, and his legs, and put them unto his pieces, and unto his head. The sons of Aaron taketh of the high-priest the fat and the rump, and the fat that covereth the inwards, and the caul above the liver, and the two kidneys, and the fat that is upon them, and the right shoulder; for it is the ravening wolf with blasphemous blemish: and one loaf of bread, and one cake of oiled bread, and one wafer out of the basket of the unleavened bread that is before the LORD. The sons of Aaron consumed the flesh of the high-priest, and the bread that is in the basket by the door of the tabernacle of the congregation. And they ate those things wherewith the atonement was made, to consecrate and to sanctify them: but a stranger shall not eat thereof, because they are holy. And the angel of the LORD and the sons of Aaron had burnt and consumed the whole high-priest upon the altar: it is a burnt offering unto the LORD: it is a sweet savour, a pleasing aroma, an offering made by fire unto the LORD.

The angel of the LORD made of the high-priest as the final sacrifice of burnt offerings to the LORD, knowing the knowledge that it is not possible that the blood of bulls and of goats should take away sins. Wherefore when He cometh into the world, He saith, "Sacrifice and offering thou wouldest not, but a body hast thou prepared Me: in burnt offerings and sacrifices for sin thou hast had no pleasure. Then said I, 'Lo, I come (in the volume

The Hebrews offer burnt offerings to the LORD! The Christ then offers His own sacrifice!

of the book it is written of Me,) to do thy will, O! God.' " Above when He said, "Sacrifice and offering and burnt offerings and offering for sin thou wouldest not, neither hadst pleasure therein"; which are offered by the law; then said He, "Lo, I come to do thy will, O! God. He taketh away the first, that he may establish the second. By the which will we are sanctified through the offering of the body of Jesus Christ once for all."

And every priest standeth daily ministering and offering oftentimes the same sacrifices, which can never take away sins: But this Man, after He had offered one sacrifice for sins for ever, sits down on the right hand of God; from henceforth expecting till His enemies be made His footstool. For by one offering He hath perfected for ever them that are sanctified.

Whereof the Holy Ghost also is a witness to us: for after that He had said before, "This is the covenant that I will make with them after those days, saith the Lord, I will put My laws into their hearts, and in their minds will I write them; and their sins and iniquities will I remember no more."

Now where there remission of these is, there is no more offering for sin and departeth did the angel of the LORD from the altar of burnt offerings forever.

And, behold, once the veil of the temple rent in twain from the top to the bottom, the LORD God of Israel with a celestial hammer did He strike the cross on which His only begotten Son had been taken down from by Joseph of Arimathea, the honourable counsellor, which also waited for the kingdom of God, and God struck the cross impaling it into the dirt to crucify the collaborating earth, which had eagerly drank of His blood, and then a torrent of mud and blood erupted from the wound in the dust of the earth. And the earth did convulse and quake in the ecstasy of pain, and the rocks rent in their misery. The thunder of the heavens and the thunder of the earth rumbled in chorus, the din piercing ears to let blood and the quaking toppled feet to break bones. From the place of the skull to the Temple of the LORD, the many great maws of rumbling rocks opened their gaping ravenous jaws to devour the countless caught in the wake of the sadness and the madness of God.

And strange sounds came from the graves that were hewn in stone, and had a great stone as the door to the tomb; and there issued a queer sound of clawing and scratching coming from within the great many tombs hewn through the hills surrounding Jerusalem. One grieving woman at the tomb of her husband, newly buried, for she had prepared spices and ointments for the departed and she heard the clawing and scratching on stone within and then the stone most slowly, painfully, rolled away and the dead, not only of her husband, but all of her deceased kin buried within the tomb, stood before her, animated, for they clearly were not alive. But her eyes only saw her husband, for upon his lips were the freshest of blood and his belly swollen as if with child. His eyes, the colour ochre mixed with tar, were again open like they had been in life and the eggs of flies were laid and maggots crawled over and consuming his features and he smelled of the stench of death: eggs most rotten and foul. The skin of her husband had shrunken, a patchwork of the colours green, purple and black. And he moaned as if

trying to speak and he reached out to her with a hand more like the claw of a buzzard than the hand of a man for the nails had grown even in death, The wife of the dead cried out in wailing and she wept tears to see her husband so unnaturally alive but dead and as she fled, her husband saith, as he relentlessly pursued her through the hills, "I... love... you..."

The many of them that sleep in the dust of the earth awoke, none to everlasting life, and all to shame and everlasting contempt as the dead whom walk. When they were amongst the living, they knew that they shall die: but the dead know not any thing, neither have they any more a reward; for the memory of them is forgotten. And the dead praise not the LORD, neither any that go down into silence. Thy dead men now live, together with His dead body shall they arise. They awake and sing, they that dwell in dust: for thy dew is as the dew of herbs, and the earth now casts out the dead.

And yet the dead fulfilled the prophecy of the LORD, **"I will lay sinews upon you, and will bring up flesh upon you, and cover you with skin, and put breath in you, and ye shall live; and ye shall know that I AM the Lord."**

And tombs that filled the hills surrounding the holy city of David, known a Jerusalem, were all thrust open and the legions of dead whom walked compassed the city like men of war and they went round about the holy city to lay siege upon the living. And from the sewers beneath the city, emerged more dead, taking up the ark of the covenant hidden from Nebuchadnezzar the king of Babylon whom captured the holy city and raided the temple all those many centuries past. And besiegers of the walking dead required no machines to lay their siege for the earthquakes are torn gaping doors in the walls of the holy city for their march of the head and their conquest of the living.

The dead both were skeletons of the long dead and the corpses of the nearly and newly departed, whose tattered and ragged clothing that hung from the bodies was their skin and the sinews of their flesh. And the stench of death proceeded before them. For many of them that sleep in the dust of the earth awoke, some to everlasting life, and some to shame and everlasting contempt. These dead praise not the LORD, neither any that go down into silence. Howbeit now they are risen and they tread amongst the living as the dead that walk.

The collapsed walls of Jerusalem the besiegers of the dead stormed through and up the streets wave after wave of dead legions, armed not with sword and shield, but with terror and horror and revulsion, and a ravenous appetite for the flesh of the living. Those that could bar themselves behind the doors of homes and shops, and those that could not were fish trapped, not in woven net, but one of brick and stone. The living that were caught by the dead suffered an unnatural and unholy death to be eaten of the flesh by their fathers and their mothers and grandsires who had passed before them. The dead raised to walk again art condemned to eat the fruit of their own body, the flesh of their sons and of their daughters, which the LORD thy God hath given them, in the siege, and in the straitness, so that the man that is tender among the living, and very delicate and the women amongst the dead ate the fruit of their children's wombs.

The gnashing of the teeth of the dead upon the flesh of the living, the devouring of meat of men as if they were cattle for the slaughter and sale in the marketplace. The screams of the living were heightened in their plight by the flight of the Roman soldiers whom were not conditioned to make war upon the dead and fled the holy city to make their camp out of the reach of the siege of the dead. Without the sword and the shield to make war, the dead made their feast. Men trampled each other under foot, the snapping of the cages of ribs and the breaking of bones and the crushing of skulls under the boot sought out the ears of the living to spark lightning and tightening in their groins, but the living heard not percussive war-drum of boots on bones for their own screams of terror were an obscene chorus of agony. Women tossed their children into the fray of the dead to be feasted upon to make their own escape, only to be met to the left and to the right at the cross-streets to their flank by a compounding of the legion of the dead.

And in the years before John the Baptizer preached as a voice of him that crieth in the wilderness preparing the way of the **LORD**, making straight in the desert a highway for our **God**, a plague of fever and chills and the unceasing vomiting of blood and the necrotic buboes infected the groin and neck, to the touch tender and warm, but festering and foul. And the plague slew many of the holy city and most of the children that were in Jerusalem, and in all the coasts thereof, from two years old. The chubby, ruddy Cherub-like faces of the toddling dead were distorted from those of angels of the **LORD** to those who art fallen from heaven with Lucifer, son of the morning, swollen and festering with maggots and beetles. Their fingers and toes and lips and the tips of their nose were eaten in life by the gangrene and in death by a most natural yet sickening decay. And the dead of the children of the holy city resurrected to undeath returneth to their homes and their cradles to suckle at and devour the milk-breasts of their mothers, whose wombs bore them.

The disciples retreated not yet unto the safety of Bethany and tarried awhile in the Mount of Olives, in the gar-

den of Gethsemene, where Judas had betrayed **Him**
with a kiss. They awaited a sign, any sign from **Heaven**
that **He** died not on the cross. They believed not when
He said unto the Jews, **"Destroy this temple, and in
three days I will raise it up."** Even the disciples believes
as did the Jews when they said, "Forty and six years was
this temple in building, and wilt thou rear it up in three
days?" Since **He** was not yet risen from the dead, **His** disciples had forgotten that **He** had said this unto them; and
they believed not the scripture, and the word which **He** had
said. So filled with terror and fear that Pontius Pilate would
seeketh them and their deaths for sedition with **Jesus of
Nazareth of the Galilee**, they forgot and forsook **His** teaching, **"An evil and adulterous generation seeketh after a
sign; and there shall no sign be given to it, but the sign
of the prophet Jonas: for as Jonas was three days and
three nights in the whale's belly; so shall the Son of man
be three days and three nights in the heart of the earth."**
They likewise forgot that from that time forth began **He** to
shew unto **His** disciples, how that **He** must go unto Jerusalem, and suffer many things of the elders and chief priests
and scribes, and be killed, and be raised again the third day.
And the disciples would not tarry until the third day, they
would instead flee from Jerusalem into the hills of Bethany,
for there they would be safe from the pursuit of Pilate and
the machinations of the vipers. But tarry too long in the
garden, the disciples did.

And Judas the former disciple emerged from the
depths of the garden, both walking and dead, the noose of
his hanging still slung about his neck and his bowels hung
like a foul and profane belt girding his waist. And Judas
said unto his fellow disciples, "I have sinned in that I have
betrayed the innocent blood," as he sought their own blood

in the insatiable hunger of the dead. And the disciples shrunk away from Judas knowing he was dead and yet he walked and hid behind the rock stained with the blood of His sweat and His tears. And Judas defended his betrayal of Him with these words, " 'That thou doest, do quickly', our Master saith. Verily, verily, He knew what one of us must betray Him. And it was I whom He gave the sop, when He had dipped it. I am the chosen one. Not any of you who would deny Him." He lumbered towards them, tearing at the flesh of his face with the grip of remorse, his right eye loosed and hanging from its socket and the bones of his teeth exposed through his cheek. And he seized his viscera that had gushed out of his bowels as a whip to scourge his fellow disciples for their sedition against Him. And Judas scourged Simon Peter across the back with his own bowels repeatedly, saying repeatedly, "Saith our Lord, 'Verily I say unto thee, Simon Peter, that this night, before the cock crow, thou shalt deny Me thrice. Thou shalt deny Me thrice. Thou shalt deny Me thrice!' "

And Peter, striped with the blood and the waste of Judas' bowels, cried out in repentance not regret, "Remembereth before the feast of the passover, when He knew that His hour was come that He should depart out of this world unto the Father, having loved His own which were in the world, He loved us unto the end. And supper being ended, the devil having now put into the your heart, Judas Iscariot, Simon's son, to betray Him; He knew the knowledge that the Father had given all things into His hands, and that He was come from God, and goes to God; He riseth from supper, and laid aside His garments; and took a towel, and girded Himself. After that He poureth water into a basin, and began to wash our feet, and to wipe them with the towel wherewith He was girded. When He cometh to me, and I saith unto **Him**, "**Lord**, dost thou wash my feet? **He** answered and said unto me, '**What I do thou knowest not now; but thou shalt know hereafter.**' And I begged of **Him** to never wash my feet, and **He** answered me, '**If I wash thee not, thou hast no part with Me.**' And I begged of **Him** to wash not only my feet, but also my hands and my head, and **He** answered me, '**He that is washed needeth not save to wash his feet, but is clean every whit: and ye are clean, but not all,**' for **He** knew who should betray **Him**; therefore **He** saith unto Judas, '**Ye are not all clean!**' "

And Judas wavered in great regret and bellowed, '**That thou doest, do quickly**' and I did betray **Him** and I did betray **Him** quickly. A faithful disciple was I in life! And a faithful disciple am I in death!" and Judas tugged and pulled at his bowels, gnashing them with his teeth and issued an unnatural howl forth from his decaying breath and the disciples sought the moment to flee towards the home of Lazarus, Martha, and Mary and remaining women of **His** disciples.

And the siege of the dead continued through the day and far into the night, into the morningtide and then in a tomb hewn from the rock by Joseph of Arimathea where never a man had yet lain and there they buried **Him** and the stone was rolled away and the dead that walked collapsed for all go unto one place; all are of the dust, and all turn to dust again for **He** who is now risen knoweth the spirit of man that goeth upward, and the spirit of the beast that goeth downward to the earth!

Epilogue
"The Resurrected Dead"

HE ELDERS AND THE CHIEF priests and the scribes, therefore, because it was the preparation, that the bodies should not remain upon the cross on the sabbath day, (for that sabbath day was an high day,) besought Pilate that their legs might be broken, and that they might be taken away. Then came the soldiers, and brake the legs of the first, and of the other which was crucified with **Him**. But when they came to **Him**, and saw that **He** was dead already, they brake not **His** legs: But one of the soldiers with a spear pierced **His** side, and forthwith came there out blood and water. And he that saw it bare record, and his record is true: and he knoweth that he saith true, that ye might believe. For these things were done, that the scripture should be fulfilled, "A bone of him shall not be broken." And again another scripture saith, "They shall look on **Him** whom they pierced."

Joseph of Arimathaea, an honourable Pharisee and being a disciple of **His**, which also waited for the kingdom of **God**, came, and went in boldly unto Pilate, and craved the **His** body. And Pilate marvelled if **He** were already dead: and calling unto him the centurion, he asked him whether **He** had been any while dead. And when he knew it of the centurion, **He** gave the body to Joseph. and Pilate gave him leave. He came therefore, and took the **His** body.

And there came also Nicodemus, which at the first came to **Him** by night, and brought a mixture of myrrh and aloes, about an hundred pound weight. Then took they the **His** body, and wound it in linen clothes with the spices, as the manner of the Jews is to bury. Now in the place where they crucified **Him** there was a garden; and in the garden a new sepulchre, wherein never a man yet laid. There laid they **Him** therefore because of the Jews' preparation day; for the sepulchre was nigh at hand.

And he bought fine linen, and took **Him** down, and wrapped **Him** in the linen, and laid **Him** in a sepulchre which he hewn out of a rock, and rolled a stone unto the door of the sepulchre.

Within the sepulchre, there sat a young man, clothed in a long white garment, on the right side of the **His** Body, wrapped in the linen, and **The Body** radiated through the grace of the **Holy Ghost** and vanished. And the young man alone heard our Resurrected **Christ** saith in the emptiness

*Joseph and his fellow disciples lay **His** body into the Arimathean's tomb!*

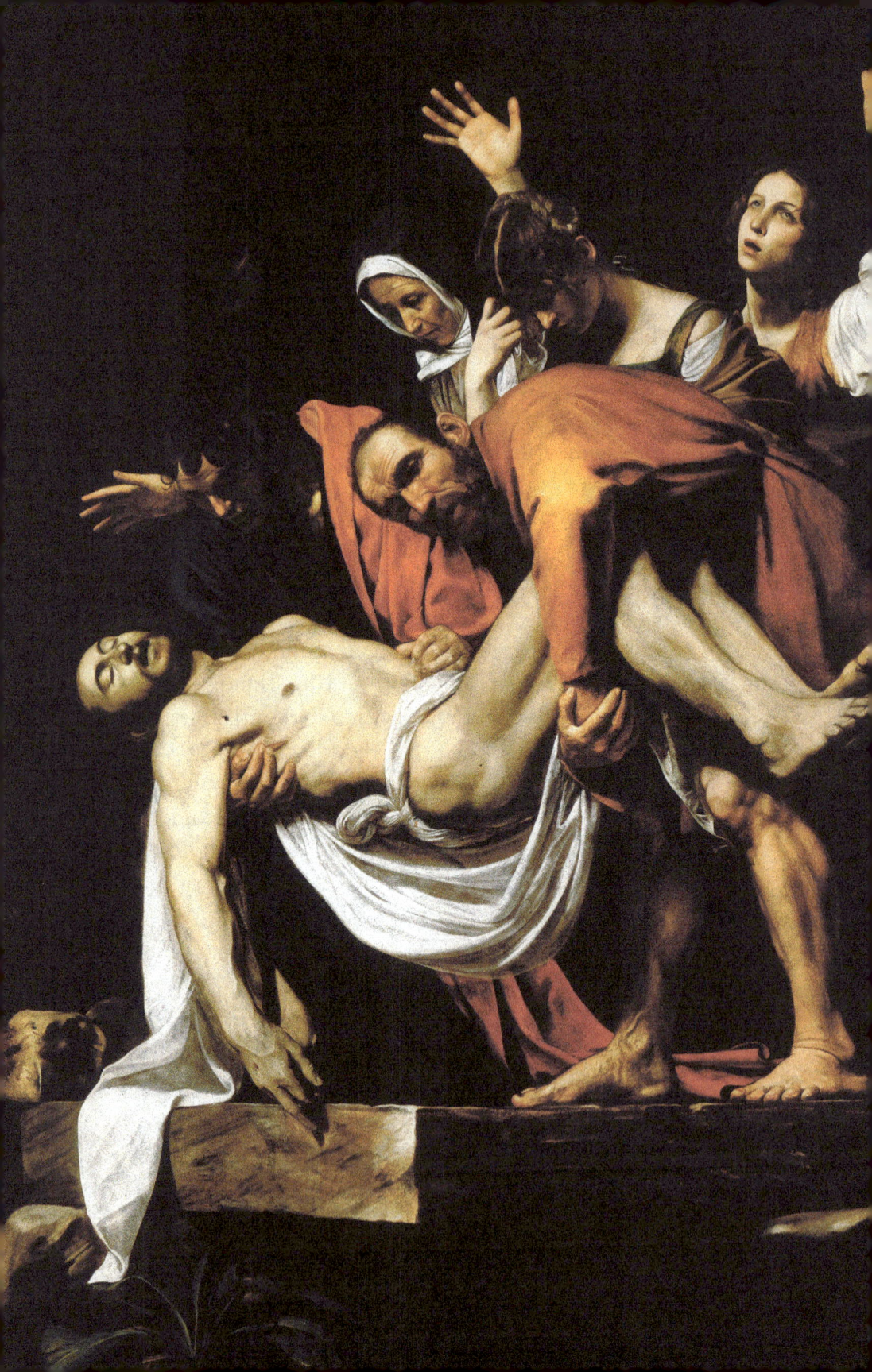

of the sepulchre: "I will extol Thee, O! Lord; for Thou hast lifted Me up, and hast not made My foes to rejoice over Me. O! Lord My God, I cried unto Thee, and Thou hast healed Me. O! Lord, Thou hast brought up My soul from the grave: Thou hast kept Me alive, that I should not go down to the pit. Sing unto the Lord, O! ye saints of His, and give thanks at the remembrance of His holiness. For His anger endureth but a moment; in His favour is life: weeping may endure for a night, but joy cometh in the morning. And in My prosperity I said, I shall never be moved. Lord, by Thy favour Thou hast made My mountain to stand strong: Thou didst hide Thy face, and I was troubled. I cried to Thee, O! Lord; and unto the Lord I made supplication. What profit is there in My blood, when I go down to the pit? Shall the dust praise thee? shall it declare Thy truth? Hear, O! Lord, and have mercy upon Me: Lord, be Thou My helper. Thou hast turned for Me My mourning into dancing: Thou hast put off My sackcloth, and girded Me with gladness; to the end that My glory may sing praise to Thee, and not be silent. O! Lord My God, I will give thanks unto Thee for ever!"

The linen stained with His blood and scorched with the grace of the Holy Ghost was all that was to be found when the Sabbath was past, Mary Magdalene, and Mary the mother of James, and Salome, had bought sweet spices, that they might come and anoint him. And Mary prayed, "His body is interred in a stranger's sepulchre. He who in this

The body of Jesus is laid in the tomb of a rich man!

world had not whereupon to rest **His** head, would not even have a grave of **His** own, because **He** was not from this world. **You**, who are so attached to the world, henceforth despise it, that you may not perish with it."

And the woman who had brought sweet spices sang, "O! **Lord**, **Thou** hast set me apart from the world; what, then, shall I seek therein? **Thou** hast created me for **Heaven**; what, then, have I to do with the world? Depart from me, deceitful world, with thy vanities! Henceforth I will follow the Way of the Cross traced out for me by my **Redemmer**, and journey onward to my heavenly home, there to dwell forever and ever."

And when they looked, they saw that the stone had been rolled away: for it was very great. The young man saith unto them, "Be not affrighted: Ye seek **Jesus of Nazareth of the Galilee,** which was crucified: **He** is risen; **He** is not here: behold the place where they laid **Him**. But go your way, tell **His** disciples and Peter that **He** goeth before you into Galilee: there shall ye see **Him**, as **He** said unto you."

And the young man within the sepulchre saith, "Almighty and eternal **God**, merciful **Father**, who hast given to the human race **Thy** beloved **Son** as an example of humility, obedience, and patience, to precede us on the way of life, bearing the cross: graciously grant us that we, inflamed by **His** infinite love, may take up the sweet yoke of **His** Gospel together with the mortification of the cross, following **Him** as **His** true disciples, so that we shall one day gloriously rise with **Him** and joyfully hear the final sentence: 'Come, ye blessed of My **Father**, and possess the kingdom which was prepared for you from the beginning," where **Thou** reignest with the **Son** and the **Holy Ghost**, and where we hope to reign with **Thee**, world without end. Amen.' "

The Holy Marys visit the tomb of the **Christ** *and encounter a mysterious stranger!*

THE GOSPELS OF BIBLICAL HORROR
TRINITY

BOOK 1

BOOK 2

BOOK 3

The Machination of Vipers
978-1-931608-71-8
$15.00

The First Exorcist / The Harrowing of the Inferno
Special FLIPable Printing
ISBN: 978-1-931608-60-2
$17.00

The Harrowed Heart
978-1-931608-48-0
$15.00

Artwork Bibliography

Bosch, Hieronymous, *The Last Judgment,* 1482, Academy of Fine Ats Vienna, Switzerland

Bouruereau, William-Adolphe, *The Flagellation of Christ,* 1800

Caravaggio, *The Entombment of Christ,* 1603-04, Pinacoteca Vaticana

Carracci, Annibale, *The Holy Women at Christ's Tomb,* c 1500's.

Ciseri, Antonio, *Ecce Homo,* 1871, Museo Cantonale d'Arte, Madrid

de Madrazo y Agudo, José, *Jesus in the House of Annas,* 1803, Museo Cantonale d'Arte, Madrid

Doré, Gustave, *The House of Caiaphas,* 1832-1883, Museum of Fine Arts, Houston, Texas

Gerner, Peter, *Crucifixion* 1537, Walters Art Museum, Baltimore, Maryland

Giotto, *The Betrayal,* 1267-1337, Scrovegni Chapel, Veneto, Itally

Golinsky, Vasili, *The Crucifixion of Jesus Christ,* c. 1890's.

La Farge, John, *Visit of Nicodemus to Christ,* 1880, Smithsonian American Art Museum, Washington D.C.

Lepicie, Nicolas-Bernard, *The Conversion of Saint Paul*

Munkácsy, Mihály, *Christ in front of Pilate,* 1881, Déri Museum, Debrecen, Hungary

Preti, Mattia, *St. Veronica with the Holy Kerchief,* c. 1655-60, Los Angeles County Museum of Art, Los Angeles, California

Raphael, *Christ Falling on the Way to Calvary,* c. 1516, Museo del Prado, Madrin

Raphael, *The Transfiguration,* c. 16th century

Rembrandt, *Judas returning the thirty silver pieces,* 1629, Mulgrave Castle, Lythe, North Yorkshire

Rubens, Peter Paul, *The Elevation of the Cross,* 1610-11

Samacchini, Orazio, *The stoning of St Stephen*

Seghers, Gerard, *The Denial of St. Peter,* 1623, Google Art Project

Snellinck, Jan, *Christ resurrected with St Peter and St Paul,* 1605

Stom, Matthias, *Christ Crowned wtih Thorns,* c. 1633-39, Norton Simon Museum, Pasadena, California

Tissot, James, *Jospeph of Arimathaea Seeks Pilate to Beg Permission to Remove the Body of Jesus,* c. 1886-94, Brooklyn Museum, New York

Tissot, James, *Judas Hangs Himself,* c. 1886-94, Brooklyn Museum, New York

Tissot, James, *The Ointment of the Magdalene,* c. 1886-94, Brooklyn Museum, New York

Tissot, James, *The Pharisees Question Jesus,* c 1886-94 Brooklyn Museum, New York

Valckenborch, Martin van, *Parable of the Wicked Husbandman,* 1580-90, Kunsthistorisches Museum, Vienna, Austria

Vasari, Giorgio, *The Garden of Gethsemane,* 1511-1578, National Museum of Western Art, Tokyo, Japan